KENNARDS VALLEY

KENNARDS VALLEY

First Published by;
Robert G George - August 2011
Reprinted and Published by Krafty Stuff - Books
April 2012

ISBN 978-0-473-18870-2

www.kraftystuff.com

Printed by LULU
www.lulu.com

CONDITIONS OF SALE

AUTHORS NOTE

This book is a book of fiction.

Any resemblance to persons dead or alive is purely coincidental.

Kennard's Valley, Standish Estate and specific addresses given are also fictional, however broader locations and towns are real, and where historical events or locations are mentioned, I have endeavoured to make these as accurate as possible. However this is not in any way intended to be a historical narrative so I apologise for any errors that may have occurred. Any psychological methodology described is also in no way meant to reflect real methodology.

Because this book has been written in, and about New Zealand, it uses some colloquialisms and terms that may not be familiar to all readers. For this reason I have included a Glossary at the end of this book.

"They will hunger no more nor thirst anymore, neither will the sun beat down upon them nor any scorching heat, because the Lamb, who is in the midst of the throne, will shepherd them, and will guide them to fountains of waters of life. And God will wipe out every tear from their eyes."

Revelation 7:16,17

STANDISH FAMILY TREE

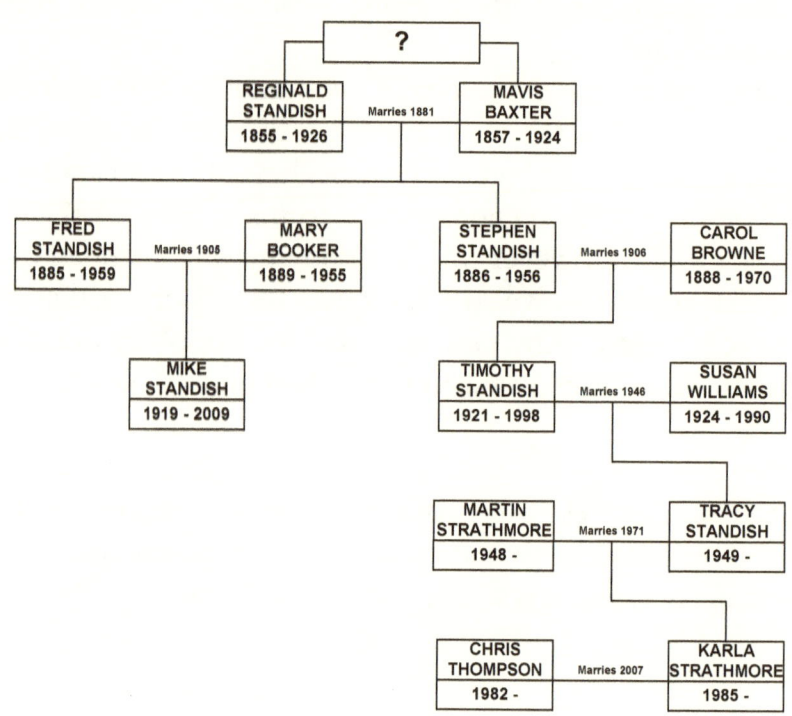

CHAPTER 1

A warm gentle breeze seemed to make the leaves tinkle in the trees at the side of the house. Autumn would soon turn them many shades of gold and brown.

From where Mike sat on the porch, he could see right across the valley to the mountains in the distance. The sun glinted on the snow that barely covered the peaks, bathing the scene with a soft orange glow. A small area of lawn led to the low wire-mesh fence that separated him from the narrow metal road that meandered up the valley, until it terminated at the Sawyers farm, another 10 km distant. The birds were in full fettle chirping out their goodnight chorus, jostling for position in the trees, and snatching a last feed of the bugs that danced and sparkled in the suns rays. Mike always loved this time of year.

The old dog gave him a gentle nudge with her nose, and then rested her head on the old man's foot.

"You're a faithful old girl, aren't ya," he said as he lent forward and scratched her head. "How many years has it been? Must be eighteen at least; no, nineteen."

He settled back into the old padded rocking chair and closed his eyes. His mind drifted back, peeling away the years. Flashes of memory, people and places paraded by. He thought back to his youth, back to his childhood and his parents. He could still remember clearly his early life as a boy of five, playing on the farm. Ninety years had past by so quickly. Happy memories: of cows and pigs and fishing in the river; of riding bikes down country lanes; of swings and tree huts. Still, he always seemed to return to one special memory. A memory that seemed half real, half dream; an illusion. But was it? For him at least, it was now a reality; but he had not always felt that way. It was 70 odd years ago, and still it seemed like yesterday. Nine days missing from his life, yet he remembered every one so vividly. Nine days that would change his destiny forever.

He shook the thoughts from his mind, and put his hand on Jess's head. "Karla and Chris are coming up tomorrow. You like Karla, don't you?" The old dog sat up at the mention of her name, looked around, then yawned and gave a little bark. "I do too; she is so much like … like…"

He stopped and closed his eyes. The evening was closing in. A small tear trickled down his cheek. "Like Paula," he said softly. He remembered the vow that they had made; that one day they would be together, forever, and it saddened him greatly that he would never fulfil his promise.

Mike sighed and stretched. "Come on old girl, let's get some grub," he said as he pushed himself to his feet, then slowly he turned and shuffled in through the door, Jess at his side.

It was far too big for him, a six-bedroom homestead on a little section. The whole thousand-acre property had once been his, but twenty years ago he had sold it off, except for the little corner that he now occupied. He had been born here as had his father before him, and he knew and loved no other place, except for the valley. He had gone to primary school in the local town of Springfield, and although that had been the extent of his scholastic education, at thirteen he was no fool. He had quickly learned how to carry out all the tasks required in running a farm, and between him, his father, and a few hired workers; they had put most of the property into pasture.

The whole farm had changed dramatically over the years, and a large picture over the fireplace showed it all.

On the left half was an aerial photo of the farm taken in 1934. On the right the same view taken in 1987. About the only thing recognisable was the area on which the farmhouse now stood.

Picking up his walking stick from where it lent against the wall beside him, Mike shuffled through the doorway and made his way across the sitting room into the kitchen. After putting another piece of wood in the coal range, he pulled down a can of dog food and rummaged for an opener.

"Jess, get your bowl girl." Obediently the old dog limped to the corner of the room and picked up the plastic container, holding it up so Mike could reach it. He scooped in a generous portion of food and held it out for her. Jess took the now half full bowl and returned it to the corner where, after giving Mike a cursory look that said thank you, she started to eat.

"You're not long for this world either are you Jess?" Mike whispered under his breath.

He made his way along the bench to the refrigerator and opened the door, putting the half full can in beside the can he had opened that morning. He sighed, and shook his head in resignation of his forgetfulness; then preparing himself a sandwich, he made his way back to the sitting room to watch the news.

"Good evening, it's six O'clock. Here is the news for February 12 2009," the presenter stated.

"Tomorrows our anniversary Jess," Mike exclaimed, rubbing her head. It was a strange anniversary. Not his wedding, or his birthday, but the day he was found lying in the now abandoned railway tunnel at the bottom of the valley across the road. He watched the television for a while longer, but his mind could not focus.

"More murders, more wars, more accidents," Mike grimaced, and then turned off the sound and picked up the book he was reading.

It was about 11pm when he woke. The room was ablaze with a flickering light from the TV. Jess lay at his feet as usual. Mike blinked his eyes and stretched, slowly becoming fully awake.

"Cuppa" he said to no one in particular, and eased his way into the kitchen. After making a coffee, he took his stick and shuffled his way back out onto the veranda again to sit in his favourite chair. From there he could see across the road through the seven-wire fence, across the valley into the darkness, and over the now invisible bush on the far side. It had been a bush reserve for as long as he could remember, a favourite walk for trampers making their way into the foothills of the mountains beyond.

A diesel train horn wailed mournfully from out of the darkness. It used to come from the valley below, but the line had been re-routed many years ago, and it now echoed from out of another valley behind him.

He thought back to that February day in 1939, and of the only woman he had ever loved; Paula.

CHAPTER 2

The third day of February was not a particularly special day in Mike's life. It was fine but overcast, and it was Sunday. That meant it was his day off from the farm. He had decided the night before that this day he would walk the track to the forest park.

He rose about 7am and put some bacon into a hot fry pan, followed soon after by a pair of fresh farm eggs. Two slices of toast dripping in butter and a cup of tea completed the meal. Now he could turn his attention to lunch.

A voice came from behind him. "Good morning, darling."

"Morning, Mum," he replied. "Sorry, did I wake you?"

"The smell of bacon woke your Father."

"Ahh, I see."

"You off soon?" Mary asked.

"As soon as I make lunch."

"I'll make you a deal then. Since you just ate the last two eggs, you get me some more from the coop, and I'll make you some lunch, OK?"

"OK."

Picking up the empty basket as he passed the end of the bench, he went out to the chicken run and soon collected eight large brown eggs. He stopped and listened to an approaching steam train, quiet and distant at first, then sound exploded into the valley as it exited the tunnel. With a smile he returned to the kitchen with his booty, feeling very content with his life. The farm and his surroundings; they were familiar and comfortable. Why wouldn't he be content?

It was a little after 8.30 when he started out down the valley to where the railway had been laid.

The Christchurch to Greymouth line was completed in August 1923 and saw quite a bit of rail traffic.

Steam was in its heyday and Mike would often lie in bed at night listening to the beat from the smoke stacks as the trains climbed the grade out of the tunnel. It was a rhythmic sound that soothed him to sleep.

He climbed the stile over the fence across the road from the farm gate, making his way down the paddock using the well-worn cattle paths until he reached the boundary fence beside the track. Coal smoke hung in the still cool air and added to the morning mist that blanketed the trees, softening both sight and sound, and creating an almost ethereal world.

Now he had two choices. He could either cross the railway, making his way up the other side to meet the walking track; that was equally as steep going up as the grade he had just come down; or he could walk down the line for approximately one mile until he got to the rail tunnel. The tunnel was 820 yards long, and by walking through it, he could meet the same walking track another 200 yards further on where it descended from the other side to the same level as the railway. Mike considered the options and although it was not necessarily the safer of the two ways, he chose the rail tunnel. 'Why climb all that way up, just to descend back to the level of the railway, ' he reasoned. Being a Sunday there was not a lot of rail traffic so he was fairly certain he would be safe. Even if a train did come, there were alcoves in the tunnel wall provided for track workers to move into, though the problem was finding them in the dark.

He set off at a brisk pace through a small cutting. The air was always heavy down here. Often in winter the mist would never leave the valley, shrouding it in mystery. When he was younger the valley had scared him. Trees made eerie noises, and he thought he saw monsters and strange creatures moving through the mist. Native orchids and creepers hung from the trees, and moss covered everything. The bush was damp and smelt of rotting wood; and yet at times the fragrance of flowers wafted on the light breeze. Mike was used to the bush and had spent many nights out in the back blocks by himself, but the valley still made him uneasy, and he stayed out of it at night. He would rather walk the extra ten miles it would take by road to get to the highway, than take a shortcut through it in the dark.

He soon broke out of the cutting and onto a raised embankment. Here the sun even managed to get a small look in, and it raised his spirits as he approached a bridge over a small stream. He stopped before crossing, and getting down onto his hands and knees, put his ear on the steel rails. "Hell that's cold," he exclaimed as he quickly lifted his head. He put his head down again, this time ready for the burn on his ear, and he listened. If a train was close he would be able to hear the rails singing, but he heard nothing. Mike made his way out onto the bridge, carefully judging the distance between the sleepers. There were no railings here, and if he stumbled or slipped on the wet wood, he could easily fall over the edge. You did not want to run across these bridges either and you definitely did not want to be caught on one with a train coming.

Once off the bridge he picked up the pace again and was soon in sight of the tunnel entrance. Now the bush started to close in on him, steep banks funnelling him in towards a solid rock wall. The tunnel entrance was not the original hole at the end of this natural canyon. The track bed he was now standing on what was once the bed of a river, and the tunnel was originally the entrance to a cave that led back into the hill. There were a lot of caves in the area, some small and not very deep, but others were said to go on for miles. The rail tunnel had followed the cave for some 200 yards before the cave had turned left and went way up into the mountain. The railway tunnel however carried on straight ahead.

It was rumoured that one of the tunnel workers who explored the caves had got lost for four days. He claimed it led to a hidden valley full of monsters, but no one actually believed him. Even if it had, it did not go anywhere now, as the tunnel was brick lined, and any side chambers were completely blocked off.

Listening to the rails again, Mike pulled his coat tighter around him and headed into the tunnel. For the first 50 yards he could see the track quite clearly, but as he pressed further on, the darkness started to engulf him. A noise up ahead brought him to a sudden halt. He strained to detect the source of the sound, slightly turning his head from side to side in an attempt to identify it. All he heard was a low moan as the wind blew through the confines of the tunnel. He moved on deeper into the darkness. Again he heard a noise, was it a scraping or a footstep? Animals would often wander into the tunnel, and it was not uncommon to find a dead sheep or goat beside the tracks. Mike was not unduly worried, but still the place made him feel uneasy, and he would be glad to get out. He had gone about 50 yards more, feeling his way along the tunnel wall when his hand disappeared in emptiness. It was one of the safety alcoves for the workers.

Suddenly, there was a sound of shifting rocks. He half turned. There was a sharp pain in his head. He felt his knees crumble beneath him. He tried to throw himself sideways into the alcove hoping that he was not on the tracks as all went blank.

CHAPTER 3

Mike woke up in darkness. Almost immediately he became aware of the pain at the back of his head. He tried to put his hands up to touch it but found he couldn't move them, then quickly discovered that he could not move his feet either. He resisted the immediate urge to panic, and instead listened, trying to take in his surroundings. Slightly to his left, and some distance away, he could make out a dull orange flickering glow in the darkness.

As his eyes began to adjust, he could just start to make out that his hands and feet were tied with rope, and he was sitting on the ground, with his back propped up against a niche in a rock. He immediately froze, now fully aware that this was no accident. He listened for any sounds. Off to his right he could hear water dripping from somewhere high above and splashing into well-worn pools, the sound almost metallic as each drop echoed loudly around the walls of the chamber.

Now, as he focused his attention, he could definitely hear movement from the direction of the light. Carefully, slowly he moved his head around to take in more of his surroundings.

He was in a natural cave, quite large, about 8 feet high and 20 feet across, and seemed to extend in front of him for some distance, before turning away to his left. The light seemed to be emanating from around that corner. Stalagmites and stalactites rose and hung respectively all around him. A slightly musty scent, reminding him of wet mud-laden leather boots, hung in the air: but this was intermingled with a more acrid smell, one resembling that of rendering fat.

He suddenly stopped, his ears straining to detect a new sound. There was someone else nearby; he could hear them moving about behind him, just the gentle rasp of material on stone. They were very close. Mike tensed, and then someone was beside him.

"You awake?" The voice was rough yet not harsh.

Mike thought for a moment but could see no reason to delay the inevitable. "Yes," he replied, letting his breath out in measured amounts, not knowing if he was about to get hit again.

"He's OK," the voice called out into the dim light.

Another male voice replied from somewhere ahead of him. "Good, let's get out of here."

There was a scuffing of feet, then footsteps echoed through the cavern. The flickering light grew stronger, and Mike was temporarily blinded as a flaming torch suddenly appeared from around the corner, obscuring the view of his second captor. In his mind he had formulated a picture of bearded powerful youths, with knives and guns, and ugly scars on their faces. He almost gasped out loud as his vision returned and he beheld an older man, slight but strong, clean-shaven and smiling.

"Welcome to Kennard's Valley," the man said kindly.

Now the man from beside him stood up and came into the torchlight. He too was elderly, in his sixties or seventies Mike guessed, he also smiled and nodded.

Mike looked at them puzzled. Could these really be kidnappers? Maybe he had fallen, and these kindly men had found him, but were scared of him, so tied him up.

"How did I get here?" Mike asked.

"We brought you here," the first one said.

"Yes, sorry we had to hit you, but we probably could not have overpowered you otherwise," added the other.

Mike sat dumbfounded. 'Have I just been kidnapped by a pair of geriatrics?' He wanted to laugh, but decided not to. Antagonising these men while he was still bound and at their mercy would not be a smart move. He decided to play their game for a while at least, until he could assess their real motives.

"Why have you brought me here?"

"More of that later. My name is Marcus, and this is Urgut," replied the man with the torch.

"Let's get you back to the farm, cleaned up and fed."

Urgut knelt down and untied Mike's feet, then one on each side they lifted him upright. The exertion caused his head to spin and he fell forward, but Marcus grabbed him and steadied him until he got his balance.

They made their way through the cave, and had not travelled far, when a slight breeze brought his attention to a side passage that disappeared into the darkness off to his left. Mike thought he could hear the sound of a distant waterfall, and he imagined the dark water, cold and deadly, racing over a precipice, to disappear unseen into a watery abyss. Falling into one of those in the dark would mean instant death with no hope of ever being discovered. He tried to keep account of the passages they were taking, making a map in his mind, but after 10 minutes he was hopelessly lost. The path was often strewn with rocks and obstacles, and in places they had to skirt around deep chasms, which disappeared into a bottomless darkness. At one of these they stopped and Marcus kicked a rock over the edge. Several seconds later, Mike heard a distant splash. Marcus looked directly at him, but said nothing. Mike however, guessed that he had done it to make a point, and he took it. In places the cave opened up into cathedral like proportions, where glow worms flaunted their eerie blue-green lights in the shadows. Their combined footsteps echoed like an army was marching through, but when they stopped; the silence was deafening.

He guessed they had travelled for nearly an hour before he became aware of a slight lightening of the walls, then coming around a corner he saw daylight. The cave entrance appeared in front of him as a large opening some 50 ft high and 100 ft across, the inside of which was covered with mosses and ferns. Birds flittered across the entrance picking off the bugs and insects that landed on a veil of flowers that hung from the roof. Just inside the opening a donkey stood grazing in a small corral. To one side was a two-wheeled open dray, and on the other was two hammocks, and an area for cooking, with an assortment of pots and pans. As they approached, the donkey looked up and brayed.

"It's OK, Seven," Marcus said softly, "it's only us and an outsider."

They stopped about 15 yards in from the cave mouth. It was very hard on his eyes looking out through the opening, but Mike could make out a long green valley dotted with trees and bushes, stretching away in the distance.

"Sorry, uh – Sorry I never asked your name," stammered Urgut a little embarrassed.

"Mike."

"Sorry Mike, but we have to blindfold you from here," said Urgut. He then took a blue scarf from his pocket, flicked it over a couple times, and tied it across Mike's eyes.

"Ouch! That's where you hit me," said Mike in a not too pleasant tone.

He loosened it a little. "Sorry."

They sat Mike on what appeared to be a pile of bags stuffed with straw, and after taking the donkey from its corral, readied the wagon for their departure. "OK," came a voice from beside him, then they lifted him to his feet and onto the back of the dray. The deck felt smooth from years of wear, and it smelt of hay, tree sap and horse. He felt the two men climb on, then two hands under his shoulders, and he was pulled forwards up against some sacks of straw.

The dray pitched forward, and a few moments later Mike felt the sun on his body. The cart seemed to turn left and they started to descend. The ground was uneven but not so bad as to throw him around too much. Occasionally they would slow right down and there would be a sideways or downward lurch as they manoeuvred around some obstacle. He started to lift his hands slowly in an attempt to sneak a look out from under his blindfold.

"Please don't do that," came a firm but pleasant command.

Mike put his arms down again, and concentrated on what he could discern through his other senses. He estimated that it had taken them about twenty minutes to reach the valley floor. He had felt the sun on the left side of his face as they had turned left out of the cave, and it had changed from being front on, to being on the side of his face five or six times, indicating that they had twisted and turned a number of times, possibly meaning that it had been quite a steep descent. Now that they were on the flat, it was on the back of his neck. He pictured the scene as he had viewed it from within the cave, mentally calculating the turns. 'OK,' he concluded silently. 'We're heading up that valley directly away from the cave mouth.'

Mike swore as he was suddenly pitched back against the seat, hitting his already sore head. He pushed himself harder in against the straw bags as the dray bounced and pitched violently. There was a splashing of hooves in water, then the sound of it rushing around them. He had been so absorbed with his re-creation of the preceding events, that he had not even noticed the approaching river. He could feel the wagon being buffeted about, and at one point he thought the donkey had lost its footing in the torrent. They splashed on for some time before they lurched up the other side on to the level.

Now they were picking up the pace, and the ground was smoother, possibly a road, and probably dirt, as he could not hear any metal under the wheels. He caught the smell of flowers. What sort he tried to think, but could not place them, but he noted their sweet smell. Time was becoming more and more difficult to estimate, but they had travelled a considerable distance when they slowed again. This time he heard the sound of a stream running across pebbles, before the splash of the donkey's hooves, as they crossed. This was a not a deep creek, and as they moved off he also noted that the sound of the water stayed on his left for about 10 minutes before either they, or the creek veered off. He listened for any other familiar sounds, tractors, machinery, airplanes, cars or trucks, but heard nothing. He thought about what Marcus had said. An "outsider" - that's what he had called him, but an outsider from where? A village; or maybe a valley? Perhaps they thought he was from a rival clan. The whole situation was bizarre; like being back a hundred years in the past in a story about feuding families and the "Wild West."

Mike slumped back onto the sacks and wondered what his future would hold.

CHAPTER 4

Sitting on the dray with no vision, had left Mike with little concept of time. It felt like they had been travelling for hours, when he suddenly became aware of a new environment. It had become colder, and where before he had not taken any notice of the clip-clop of the donkey's hooves, now they were more prominent. He felt a closeness around him, and he knew that they were no longer in open country.

'A canyon maybe?' he thought. The creaking of branches and a faint rustling of leaves soon corrected him. He listened for the sound of forestry, but nothing disturbed the peace of the trip.

He had given up trying to plot the path they were taking, and could only guess that they were still heading away from the cave.

He thought about the cave. He was not sure if he had been abducted and taken there, or was there an entrance to the cave system from the tunnel? If so, it was also possibly his way out. Suddenly the location of the cave took on a whole new urgency. Slowly Mike lifted his still tied hands and slid up the bottom of the blindfold.

"You can take it off now," said the voice behind him.

Cautiously, almost sheepishly for having been caught again, he slid it right off over his head. He quickly scanned for any sign of the cave. It must have been visible for some distance he reasoned given the size of the entrance, but all he saw was the forest they had just passed through receding behind him. Directly beyond that he guessed the valley must have stretched on for miles. To his left, about one mile away, mountains rose from the valley floor partly covered by the trees. To his right, the forest continued on until it started to ascend from the foot of the mountains. These mountains were walls of rock that rose thousands of feet high, and were capped with snow. Native bush covered the lower slopes until it gave way to Black Beech, and finally snow grass with small bushes clinging on in the less steep places. Mike tried to recollect any area around the farm like it, but nothing he could think of even remotely matched that grandeur of this place, and he thought he knew the Alps well. The country they were passing through was green and fertile. Cows and sheep grazed in the unfenced meadows. Birds danced through the trees, and buttercups filled the paddocks. It was breathtakingly beautiful, and for a moment Mike almost forgot his predicament. Then with a lurch the cart turned off the dirt track and soon came to a stop outside a fairly substantial log cabin.

Marcus and Urgut got off. Urgut untied his hands and stepped quickly back as if he expected Mike to hit him. Mike knew however, that he had a much better chance of escaping if he befriended them, so he just slid off the back and surveyed his surroundings.

Before him the valley stretched out beyond a small plantation of trees that protected the homestead from wind. To his right was a corral with a number of horses, a mixture of Clydesdales and some other breeds he could not determine. Beside that was a stable and barn with a smaller shed attached. Chickens ran loose in a fair sized coop and ducks wandered freely about the place. Mike now turned his attention to the house. It was a single story, and fairly sizable.

He had seen logs cabins before, and this was not professionally built. The logs, although de-barked, were not evenly sized, and although an effort had been made to reshape them, they did not fit very well. The gaps were filled with what looked like a mix of small pieces of wood and tightly wedged stones caulked with clay, and the roof appeared to be rough sawn timber, covered with bark shingles. The front door opened outward and was made of heavy wooden slabs fastened with wooden pegs and swung on wooden hinges. At the back, directly opposite the door, he could see the top of a stone chimney, and to the right, on the end of the building was a smaller chimney from which issued a trail of smoke. Mike could not see past the left end of the building, but it appeared to go on further past the main room.

Between the house and the barn, was a covered wagon and two 4 wheel carts. Inside the barn were a plough and till, both horse drawn. He was quite used to working with horses. Many of the farms around New Zealand still used Clydesdales or bullock teams to work the ground and cut hay, tractors were in the minority, and in many cases a novelty, but this place was different. Mike had been trying to work out what was not right, and looking about it finally dawned on him. There was no modern technology, no motors or engines, only horsepower. The equipment that was here: the wagons, the plough, were all of his grandparent's era both by design and construction.

His attention was drawn back to the house as the door opened. There stood an elderly woman, older that the two men. A long faded and patched floral dress covered her tall stocky frame. A white knitted shawl was draped over her shoulders, and a pair of what appeared to be sheep skin slippers graced her feet. She looked him up and down for a moment, then smiled briefly as she beckoned them all inside. Mike hesitated. This had to be the weirdest abduction he had ever heard about. It was like they were welcoming a neighbour or invited guest into their home. Urgut came up behind and put his hand on Mikes shoulder, then with a friendly nod ushered him in.

The door he had come through opened into a room that ran almost the whole width of the house. To the right was a curtained doorway, leading into the room with the small chimney, the kitchen he presumed. On either side of a large stone fireplace, two windows looked out to a clear area that had a washing line strung across it. A tea tree pole, cut off just above the fork of two branches, acted as a prop to keep it well off the ground, a few items hung there gently moving in the now late afternoon breeze. A pile of split logs sat on the hearth to one side. Above the fireplace was a painting of a group of 10 people. Mike stared at it for a few moments. He could definitely pick out the old woman, although she was a lot younger then. He could also now see that the building extended in an L shape to the left, and at the far end of the room, diagonally opposite from where he stood, another curtained doorway lead into the other part of the house. 'Bedrooms,' Mike thought. To the right of the doorway was a bookcase with a number of what looked like old novels and an assortment of papers made up into bundles. None of the windows had glass, but all had wooden shutters on the outside. The room smelt slightly of soot and dry grass, but rough earthenware jars of fresh flowers had been placed about, each adding their own perfume, and there was the unmistakable smell of baking bread permeating the air. Wooden chairs with canvas seats were dotted about the walls, and in the centre of the room was a large rectangular solid wooden Rimu table, obviously hewn by axe. About that were 10 chairs, also wood, and with deep blue cushions.

Marcus pulled out one of the chairs, the second from one end, and indicated that he should sit.

"Please," he said with a friendly smile.

Mike was starting to become wary at the kindness he was being shown. Was this a front to lower his guard, make him feel at ease so they could attack him? 'But that doesn't make sense either,' he thought. 'They have already attacked me, bound me, and kidnapped me. They could have killed me at any time; what is going on here?' He decided to play the friendly game in kind, but would watch his back, until something started to develop …

"Thank you," he said politely and sat down. Urgut sat just to the left of him and Marcus took up position at the end of the table. The old woman sat opposite Urgut, and looking over Mike's shoulder called out; "Paula, can you bring in food and drinks, please."

After a few moments, the curtain parted. A young woman about Mike's age came in carrying a tray of bread and assorted bowls of food. As she looked up from the fare she was carrying she caught sight of Mike and froze. She was a pretty girl with a natural beauty, and no makeup to hide it. Long auburn hair flowed down to the middle of her back. She was not tall, about 5 ft 5 inches and slim but solidly built. A purple apron covered an open neck short sleeved white shirt, and halfway down a light blue plain skirt, that almost touched the ground. As Mike watched her he could see a flood of different emotions wash over her; fear, shock and finally a look of desperation, or maybe hope, flashed across her lightly tanned face. She sat the tray by the old woman and then disappeared back through the curtain, only to re-a merge with another tray this time containing an earthenware jug and some cups. The girl stood at the end of the table, her eyes fixed downwards.

"Sit, please," the old lady said, indicating to the chair beside Mike.

The girl shuffled slowly to the seat. Without thinking Mike stood and pulled the chair out for her. Again she froze. Then hesitantly she sat down without looking at him.

'Why is she so afraid of me?' Mike wondered as he sat back down.

The old lady took a loaf and broke a piece off, before passing the bowl around to the others. They sat in a somewhat uneasy silence for about a minute before Mike spoke.

"Well, what am I doing here? You must have kidnapped me for a reason," he said.

"All in good time" replied the old woman, "all in good time, but first let us introduce ourselves. You are Mike, I believe?"

Mike nodded.

"I am Gran. Everyone calls me Gran, and you have met two of my sons, Marcus and Urgut. This," she said, nodding towards the young woman, "is Paula. She is to be your wife."

CHAPTER 5

"What!" exclaimed Mike, standing bolt upright and knocking over his chair, "You can't just kidnap somebody and expect them to marry your daughter, it's…"

"Oh, she's not my daughter, she's an outsider, just like you," cut in Gran.

Mike stood in stunned silence.

"Yes, they kidnapped me too," Paula said quietly.

Mike looked down at her angrily. She looked scared and helpless, almost trembling. He could see she was close to tears. She glanced fleetingly up at him, and then returned her stare to the table. He stood there defiantly for a while; then guessing he was probably half the reason for her discomfort, he retrieved his chair, and slowly sat down.

"Let's all have some more food and drink," said Gran. "Then, I will tell you all about why we brought you here."

Mike realised that ranting on was not going to improve, or speed up the situation. He took another slice of bread from the platter and spooned on some jam. They ate quietly for some time, each occasionally looking at the other, trying to gauge their feelings. Mike deliberately did not to look at Paula, and he felt that she was doing the same, looking like a couple of young kids tying to pluck up courage for a first date. Only much more was at stake than that. Both desperately wanted to talk, but a forced marriage between them was something neither wanted to contemplate.

Finally, Gran pushed herself back from the table and fixed her eyes on Mike.

"How old do you think I am?" she asked. Mike squirmed, and cleared his throat nervously. Women's ages were never a subject for discussion, especially when they were present.

Gran smiled, "It's OK, say what you feel, I won't mind." Mike considered her for a moment. She looked about eighty he thought, but a look in her eye, and the way she moved, made him unsure. He took a punt. "Eighty two."

"Very close, eighty three actually." She smiled again as she saw the look on Mikes face, as he looked around the room, and up at the picture. "Yes that's me, and my parents. My mother painted it. She was an excellent artist don't you think?" Mike nodded. "She painted all the portraits and scenes for everyone in the valley."

"There are more of you?" he asked surprised.

"There used to be."

"How long have you been here?"

"We arrived in this country; that is my parents did, in 1836. We found this valley shortly after by accident and have been here ever since." She let out a sigh and turned her gaze to the window. "There were actually three families that found this valley. We were settlers, farmers, brought out here and allocated land by the government. We expected to find pastures and fields, but what we got was bush. We were lost."

Mike nodded with understanding. When his grandparents, Mavis and Reginald Standish, had emigrated from England in 1878, they too were part of the New Zealand Government initiative to provide settlers with blocks of land. However, unlike the majority of those who came for a "better life" and had nothing; they had made the move fully aware of the problems they might face. They were from a generation of farmers, and had sold their one hundred acre dairy farm for a tidy sum. They were able to have a house built, and after paying the land deposit and purchasing some stock, still had enough over to support them over the months following. Even so the initial shock of moving from green meadows to dense New Zealand bush had been traumatic.

"Then some of the boys started exploring the cave systems that cover this area." Gran continued. "Two of the boys went missing, and we searched for them for days. Then just as we were about to give up we found them, or they found us, not really sure which. Anyway they said that they had found a beautiful green valley and so we all went for a look. We decided as a group to see if we could get this land, but when we searched the titles, the maps, records; we could not find it. So we decided that as no one else was here, we would just settle down until we were told to leave. We had very little in the way of possessions, so getting in through the cave system posed no problem, and the more we explored this place, the more we loved it. We bought up farming equipment, some sheep and cattle and transported them in. Once we had what we needed, we concentrated on building."

Mike glanced around the room. The floor was made of flat river stones that had been laid like cobblestones, and cemented in with what looked like a mixture of straw and clay. Over that were spread cowhides and sheepskins. Mike found it rustic, but homely at the same time. He looked back at Gran and saw she was smiling.

"Yes, that took many months, she said. "Then some of our lads ventured out. When they returned they told us that the police and authorities had declared us all dead. We then had two choices. Either we went back and told our story; that would have meant that valley would be invaded; or stay here in peace."

"But surely you knew you would be found out eventually?"

"Well that's the strange thing. We have been here over 100 years, and no one has found us yet."

Mike opened his mouth to speak, but Gran raised her finger and he stopped.

"We have never found a way out of this valley either, except through the cave system."

"But you must have been seen by aircraft flying over, I mean this is a huge valley, it must be visible from miles away."

Gran looked at him quizzically. "Aircraft?" Then she looked at Paula.

Almost painfully the girl raised her head and turned to Mike. "There are no aircraft, not even the distant sound of one. There is nothing from... from... our world. I don't think this place actually exists." Mike was about to retort, "Rubbish!" The look of anguish in her face stopped him instantly. Instead he said softly, "It exists. You're here. I'm here. We exist." Paula gave him a weak smile, then with tears welling up in her eyes, quickly looked away.

Gran spoke again. "We had been living here about ten years when we discovered the plant. We found it growing near a spring about 3 miles further up the valley," she said. "Nothing like we had ever seen before; and it grows nowhere else in the valley. We thought it might be good to eat, and it was; at least the fruit was. It made us feel happy, so we just kept on eating it." She stopped and sighed. "It took about 10 more years before we realised ... realised what had happened." Again she sighed.

Unexpectedly she stood up, and without another word, walked out the door. They all watched her go; then Marcus gave Urgut a flick of his head, indicating that he should follow her. "She finds it hard to talk about it," he said.

Mike turned and looked directly at Paula. This time she lifted her head and met his gaze. "How long have you been here?"

"About two years," she said, her voice sounding a little more relaxed.

"Have they treated you well?"

"Yes, very well." He could tell by her voice that she meant it, and was not just trying to please Marcus, who was obviously listening.

She pulled a tattered handkerchief from her apron pocket and wiped her eyes and nose. She had dreaded this day. The day a man would come to take her. She feared that she would be forced into a loveless arrangement, where she would be used as a whore, raped, and treated as a slave; nothing more that a baby making machine. Her initial fears that Mike might mistreat her were however fading slightly, and she thought that maybe she could grow to at least like him. However, she was also aware that she was desperate for the company of a person her age, male or female, for news of the outside world, and of her family that she missed so much. She knew that her judgment might be clouded.

The door opened, and Gran came in followed by Urgut. She looked over at Marcus, and the worried look on his face. "Oh fush," she said. Nothing missed her eye, and even Mike had to smile quietly to himself.

The initial shock of their first meeting having subsided, he no longer felt fearful for his life. Now he was intrigued and fascinated by this family who it seemed, time had forgotten. He expected Gran to continue her story, but instead she said, "It's getting on, we had better sort out your room. Paula, will you take Mike to the one next to you."

Paula nodded to Gran, and then looked at Mike as she stood up. Her eyes scanned his, trying to assess his feelings and motives. He looked directly back into hers. No malice, or lust, or hurt, showed there, and she gave him a tentative smile. "This way," and she made her way through the curtain.

Mike found himself in a hallway. Directly across from the curtain they had just exited through, was a door. "That's my room," she said. They carried on to the next. "This is yours." She lifted the latch and pushed it open. It was a plain square room with a shuttered window in the far wall, a bed to the left, and a table and chair made from tea tree on the right. On the table was an earthenware jar containing some dry flowers. The bed was a timber frame with a sack slung between, and a straw mattress. There was also a cushion that served as a pillow. Stacked on the end of the bed were a number of blankets.

"I'm sorry it isn't more comfortable, I'll get you some fresh flowers tomorrow," she said.

"It will be fine, thank you," Mike replied, at the same time realising the irony of the statement. This was basically his prison cell.

"Those across the other side are Gran and the boys. If you go to the end through the far door, there is a long-drop toilet outside. I'll come and get you when dinners ready". She turned to leave; then looked back with tears streaming down her face.

"Please don't run away, not without me, I beg of you," she paused and added softly "Please don't hurt me."

Mike took her hands. She was trembling. "I won't, I promise," he said quietly.

She gave him a weak smile, and wiping her eyes with her apron, ran back to her room.

Mike shut the door, and noted that there were no locks. Moving across the room he opened the shutters. The late afternoon sunlight streamed in, and he took in the vista. It was beautiful. A river, green meadows covered in flowers, the clear mountains in the distance, birds and butterflies, cows quietly grazing on the lush pastures - 'Maybe Paula is right. Maybe this isn't real. Maybe I have died, and this is paradise,' he suddenly thought. 'Well if it is, then it's living up to expectation.'

He went over to the bed, and after spreading out a blanket, lay down. He put his head on the pillow, and closed his eyes.

CHAPTER 6

He was not sure how long he had slept, when he heard a gentle knocking. He opened his eyes and found that it was quite dark. The knock sounded again, this time the catch lifted and the door slowly opened. Flickering light gradually spilled into the room, then Paula's face appeared around the edge. The look of apprehension on it made Mike sit bolt upright.

"What's wrong, what's happened?"

At his words her shoulders slumped and her face relaxed. "Thank you," she said. "Thank you for still being here, I was so scared that you would slip away."

Mike stood up and crossed the room, "I promised you I wouldn't, and I meant it," he said softly   putting his hand on her shoulder.

Paula looked him in the eyes, scanning for any deceit. "Dinners ready come and get some," she said. 'Maybe, just maybe I can trust this man,' she thought as they left.

He followed her back down to the main room. Marcus and Urgut were sitting in their seats chatting quietly. Gran was nowhere to be seen. They stopped talking as he came in and gave him a cheery smile. Marcus stood and pulled a chair out for him.

"How are you feeling?" he asked.

"My head is very tender, and I have a headache," Mike said without smiling. He was getting a bit annoyed with this game, and wanted to get back to the farm. He had work to do, and by now his parents would be getting worried. But now he had another concern: Paula. Obviously, she also wanted to get back to her family. Two years she had been here she had said. 'Had she not tried to escape?' he thought.

The curtain opened and Gran came in. The boys stood respectfully, and Mike followed suit. She gave them a nod and a smile, then Urgut pulled out her chair, and she sat down.

"What's the plan for tomorrow," she asked.

"To go home," Mike replied quickly but calmly.

"You are home!" Gran said equally calmly.

There was a long silence then the curtain opened and Paula appeared carrying a plate of steaming vegetables. She looked around at the silent faces, but her eyes fastened on Mike. He gave her a reassuring smile, and she disappeared again, returning with a pot of still bubbling stew. She moved around beside Mike who immediately stood and pulled out her chair for her. She hesitated for a moment, and looked across at Gran, who smiled and nodded for her to be seated.

"Marcus, please," Gran said.

Marcus stood and bowed his head. "Lord, we thank you for the food before us and this precious land, and the peace we have, and for our new family member, through Jesus name. Amen." He sat down, and reached for the vegetables. "Any more of that delicious bread Paula?" he asked.

"I'll see," she said, and went out quickly, returning with a platter of sliced bread and a bowl of homemade butter.

They sat and ate a meal like any family. The boys talked about cutting down an old tree for firewood. Gran would put in a word or two, but Mike and Paula sat in silence, listening and exchanging the odd glance. At the end of the meal, when Urgut finally pushed back his plate after his third helping, Paula started to get up to clear the table.

"No, please sit dear," said Gran. "That meal was delicious as usual, I don't know what I would do without you, but you need to hear this too. I have never told you the whole reason we brought you here."

"Kidnapped her you mean," cut in Mike.

Under the table, Paula put her hand on his, and gave it a squeeze; indicating that he should be silent. Mike complied, but also noticed that she did not remove it.

"As you will," Gran continued, "Like I said before, we occupied the land, three families. The Williams family had the area from the other side on the forest down to the ca…" She hesitated a moment, "down to the caravan crossing at the lower stream. The Richardson's had the area from where the river crosses the valley about two miles up from here, upstream to the head of the valley, and for the full width. Then there were us: the Kennards. There was my father Reginald, my mother Martha, and myself. We occupied this area from the forest to the river where it crosses the valley, and the full width between the other two. There were never any boundaries, and we shared everything. The Williams grew crops, the Richardson's grazed sheep and milked cows; we had cattle and a slaughterhouse. We were just one big extended family each with our own part to play. Twenty-one we were in total, and we all got on very well. We decided to take brides from among the families and live our perfect existence, cut off from the world. I took one of the Richardson's; John, as my husband; the boy's father. He died about 4 years ago." She hesitated, "Then we found the berries."

"Don't stop please Gran," Paula encouraged.

Gran nodded. "The berries as I have said were just a nice relaxant; what we did not know until about ten years after, is that the berries were making us all infertile. Urgut and Marcus were the last to be born." She stopped and put her head in her hands.

Marcus stood up and put his hands on his mother's shoulders. Mike put his hands behind his head and leaned back in his chair. "Ahh..." he said, a slight smile of comprehension on his face. Paula looked quizzically at him, but it was Gran who spoke.

"You see that's why we need you," she said looking at Paula. "We are the last of the inhabitants; we need you, who have not eaten the berries, to keep the valley alive; to carry on when we are dead."

Paula stared at Mike.

"What if we don't want to stay?" Mike said. "What's to stop us walking out tomorrow, or next week, or when you are dead," his voice challenging.

"The valley," said Marcus. Then in reply to the astonished look on Mike face, "I know what you're thinking, and you're right, the valley does not need us, we need it. Even now it has touched your heart. Its majesty, peacefulness, and its whole presence. In a very short time, you will love this valley like we do. You will never want to leave. Even Paula has fallen in love with it."

Mike looked at her. She lowered her head and shut her eyes. "But we have family, friends, a life outside of the valley, beautiful as it is, this is not our home."

"But it will be. You see there is no way out. We have explored the mountains for 100 years, and we always end up back here. Every path, trail and pass; all just turns us around and brings us back. I suspect the same is true if you wanted to come in from the outside too, that's why nobody has ever found us."

"But we got in through the caves."

"Yes, and it is the only way."

"Then we just go out the same way."

Marcus sighed. His face took on a pained look as he turned his gaze out the window. He sat in silence for a minute, then turned and looked straight back at Mike. "I'm sorry, we have to protect our valley; we can't let you."

"Like I said, if not tomorrow, then when you are too feeble to stop us."

Marcus shook his head. "Then you must first find the caves and the correct path, then find and get around the booby traps we have set." Annoyance becoming clearly evident in his voice. "We have to protect the valley, we cannot let you go, and besides, by then you will have grown to love it, and it will be yours and your children's forever."

Paula let out a little cry and put her head in her hands. Mike put his arm around her, and she sobbed.

Marcus suddenly stood up. "We," and he gestured all around the room making it clear that he included Mike and Paula, "have an obligation to protect this place. Can you imagine the tragedy it would be if the outside world got hold of it? How long before they ruined it?" He stood, hands on hips, staring confrontationally at Mike.

Mike returned his fixed stare. Every impulse was to jump up and rant and rave about how unjust this was. It was illegal; it was criminal; it was immoral; it was …; but he just held Paula, and kept silent. Seconds passed, though it seemed like minutes, then Gran purposely cleared her throat.

He looked across at her, saw the anguish on her face too, and he knew she understood. The boys too, he guessed were hurting, they must have been dreading this talk for a long time.

"Let's go outside," Mike said to Paula, while glaring back at Marcus. They stood up, and he guided her through the door and out onto the porch.

Paula led him across the dirt courtyard to a seat under a tree that looked out over the valley. The view with the moonlight sparkling on the river was breathtaking. It was a truly idyllic scene. He breathed in the fresh cool air, the scent of wild flowers, the last chorus as the birds settling down for the night, and he understood what Marcus had been talking about. They sat for a while in silence.

"What are we going to do?" Paula tentatively put her head on Mike shoulder so she could whisper in his ear.

"We have to find a way out. You must know them fairly well by now. Do you think they may be lying about no way out except through the caves?"

"No, I don't think they are. I know nobody has gotten in, so I guess the reverse is true."

"And the booby traps?"

"I don't know, but they are certainly capable."

"Then I guess we have to believe that's true also."

Mike considered the options for a moment. "We may get only one chance at this, so we had better get it right. We know the caves do lead out, so I think that would be best, what do you think?"

Mike felt her nod her head. "Do you have any idea where the caves are?" he asked.

"I am sure they are down the valley, but I don't know where. I think more than two days walk."

"I agree. When they brought me in, we approached from down stream. I know we came through a forest, and across a very flat shallow stream. I also know they are up quite high over looking the valley, and the path up is on an angle, so the drop off must be quite steep."

"Do we go tonight?" asked Paula.

"No, we need to get some supplies together, and I know they will be watching tonight. Tomorrow we'll have more time to think out our strategy. We'll go the night after possibly, but let's watch tonight to see what they do, and how they are planning their surveillance."

"What do we need to take?"

"Food and water for at least four days. Some rope and a pick or something, torches for in the caves, and warm clothing."

"The food, water and torches are easy, but the other stuff will be in the barn."

"Don't worry I will look for those tomorrow, let's go to bed, and think about anything else we may need."

Paula sat up and nodded, then, putting her hand on his she gave it a quick squeeze. They both got up and walked back indoors.

Gran and the two boys were still sitting at the table. Gran was reading and the boys played cards.

Mike knew that they had been watching them; Gran's book was upside down. They said good night and made their way to their respective bedrooms. As they stopped at Paula's door, she turned to look at him. "Thank you," she said, and went inside. Mike stood there for a while; he was getting to like this lonely girl. He went to his room, and opened the shutters. He was thankful of the little sleep he had earlier, for this night he wanted to be awake.

It was a couple of hours later when he heard subdued voices and the movement of feet in the corridor outside. The noise stopped outside his door and he could see a flicker of light from underneath. I had better give them something to listen to he thought. So he gave a snort, and turned over as noisily as he could. The light disappeared, and he heard a door latch, once, twice...

"OK," he muttered, "Two in bed, one on watch."

Shortly after, there was a scrape from outside the window. A shadow filled the room, and then disappeared. Mike waited a minute or two listening, but there was no other sound of movement. Quietly he got up and sneaked a look outside. There was no one in sight, so he stuffed his spare blankets under the sheets and sat back against the wall just to the side of the window. Another hour past before he heard someone approach. He looked and saw a head just sneak a look in at his bed, then obviously satisfied, move away again. Mike stood up and carefully looked out. He could see a figure moving away towards the front of the building. Carefully, quietly, he slipped out of the window and followed. The figure moved to the seat where he and Paula had sat earlier and leaned back contentedly. Quietly he retraced his steps back to the house. He stopped at Paula's window and listened, but there was no sound from within. He suddenly felt very lonely, and had an almost overwhelming desire to knock on the shutters, and to hold her in his arms. He had raised his hand halfway up before he caught himself. 'Don't be so stupid.' he muttered angrily under his breath. 'You don't know this girl, you're behaving like a lovesick child. Once we get out, you will probably never see her again, and besides …,' he took a deep breath as he regained control over his emotions, 'and besides you don't want to frighten her off.' That thought somewhat shocked him, and he was still musing over it as he climbed back into his room and slipped under the covers.

CHAPTER 7

Mike was awake soon after dawn. Light streamed into the room through the open shutters.

"Good morning," a voice said.

"Good morning," Mike replied, as he squinted to look at the shadowy figure that now obscured part of the frame. His eyes soon adjusted so he could make out the face of Marcus standing there yawning.

'Just finished his shift, and making his final check,' thought Mike. "I'm still here," he said pointedly. Marcus said nothing, just smiled and moved away.

"Oh by the way, breakfast is nearly ready," said the disappearing voice.

'Breakfast; Paula; she must have been up for at least an hour to get a fire going and to have something ready. He got up, and headed out his door. Mike realised that she had to be very capable. Milking cows, making butter, cheese and bread, all by hand, and with no technology to speak of.

The smell of toast and porridge greeted him as he pushed through the curtain into the main room. A little butterfly circled around inside his stomach as he crossed the empty room towards the kitchen. "Stop that," he admonished himself as he approached the curtain, and with a deep breath pushed it aside.

"Stop what?" Paula asked as he entered.

"Oh ahh ... just talking to myself," Mike stammered not realising that he had even spoken it out loud. "How are you today?" he quickly added in an attempt to re-direct the subject.

"I'm good," she replied and smiled at him, quite differently from the tentative scared smiles he had seen the night before.

For the first time he actually looked at her properly as she squatted in front of an open fireplace. She was quite attractive he decided. Her skin was smooth and lightly tanned. A few girlish freckles dusted her cheeks and nose. Her arms were long and slim, but strong. He could see her muscles flexing as she worked a wooden spoon through the thickening porridge. Her face was longish, her features fine and almost delicate. She had the most intense deep green eyes he had ever seen, and he found himself staring into them. Suddenly he realised that he was staring into them.

"Is something wrong she asked?"

Mike cleared his throat awkwardly. "Sorry, I was just … um … you have such beautiful eyes," he blurted out. Paula blushed and turned away to continue buttering a plate of toast. 'Damn,' thought Mike. "Look I'm sorry, I didn't intend to make you feel embarrassed. I'll go and sit down."

"No," came the reply a little too quickly. She hesitated, "You can help me carry some stuff out … that is if you don't mind?" She smiled back at him as she gestured to the large bowl on the table, her blush completely gone.

"No problem," and picking it up, he pushed sideways through the curtain and carried it out. 'Phew, that was …'

"Good morning Mike." He stumbled slightly, nearly dropping the pot.

"Morning Gran," he replied recovering from the start she had given him, and wondering how long she has been sitting there. He set the pot down on the table as Paula came up behind him with the bowls and then circled the table, putting one down at each persons place. The others, he noted, had a wide spacing between them, she put his and hers much closer together. He glanced up at Gran and knew instantly that she had noted it also. 'That's good,' he thought. 'We will lull them into believing that we are getting to like each other and then they may not feel the need to watch us so closely, and that will make it easier for us to escape. We do have to trust each other at the very least.'

The door opened and the two boys came in.

"Beauty!" exclaimed Urgut as he set eyes on the table, "I don't suppose that …"

"There is any toast? Yes its coming," cut in Paula, then with an upward flick of the head, and a "tut," she disappeared back into the kitchen.

"Did you have a good sleep," asked Gran pleasantly.

"Yes thanks," and then just because he felt a bit cheeky added, "But there was something moving around outside quite a bit, a cow I suspect." He wanted to look at the boys, but instead turned around towards the kitchen as Paula re-emerged with a plate of steaming toast. She looked quizzically at him, seeing the smirk on his face. "Oh look, here is the toast," he said.

There were a few moments of silence while Paula sat down. She glanced at him with a "What's going on," kind of frown, and it took him all his willpower not to burst out laughing.

Gran saved the situation by asking Marcus to say grace.

Mike sat with his hands on his knees, and then felt another hand on top of his. He slowly turned his palm to the side and Paula's hand slid into his and she slightly clenched it. They said Amen, but the hand remained for some time before they had to release each other to eat.

"What are you two up to today," Gran asked, looking at the boys.

"Could you give me a quick tour of the place?" Mike asked Urgut quite deliberately. Urgut he decided, was the milder of the two, and therefore easier to manipulate, and besides that, he found he actually liked the man. They could easily have become friends if the circumstances were different, he thought. Urgut, as predicted, agreed enthusiastically.

"Well, we need to cut down that old tree, and stack the rounds in the shed to dry, and then I thought we could take Mike up the valley and show him around a bit," Marcus said.

"If you go up to the rapids, you might get some fish for dinner," Paula suggested.

"What about you dear?" Gran added looking her.

"Well I have some washing to do, and bake another loaf," looking at Urgut, who grinned back with a look of abject bliss, "then …"

"Go on up with the boys," Gran cut in.

"But I …"

Gran just waved her hand dismissively and put her head down to scoop up another spoon of porridge.

After the meal was finished the men helped Paula with the dishes, then Marcus indicated to Mike to follow him outside. They stood on the porch together breathing in the sweet fresh morning air. Mike took a few moments to study him. Quite a bit taller that Mike, he was lean and lanky. His limbs were brown and sinewy, veins clearly visible on the inside of his forearms. His hands were large and strong. He wore an old straw brimmed hat, that showed many repairs, a tattered and patched cotton shirt and khaki trousers that were too big for him and were held up with a hemp rope.

'He looks just like what he is,' thought Mike 'a hillbilly farmer.'

But there was something more. Something much deeper about this man; in fact, about all of them. There was a sense of being and contentment; of total integration with their environment. He looked around the valley, and the peace was all encompassing. Suddenly the import of Marcus's words hit him. "An outsider." If it was not for the fact that they had eaten those berries, he would never have been there; or Paula, for that matter.

"What was the valley like when you arrived," he suddenly asked.

"You had better ask Gran that question," replied Marcus, "but as I understand it, pretty much the same as it is now."

"Then why do you need to look after it?"

Marcus looked at him quizzically.

"I mean, if the valley has never changed, and maybe never will, why do you need us to be here to carry on if there is nothing to do?"

"Your right." Mike started at the voice from behind him. 'How does she do that?' he thought as he turned to see Gran leaning out the window.

She continued. "The valley doesn't need us to tend it or maintain it. In fact it is us that need the valley. It sustains us and protects us." She paused; "It tolerates us."

Mike opened his mouth to speak, but a single raised finger held him. "But, the valley does need us in another way, as Marcus said yesterday. It needs our silence. It needs our protection to keep it hidden from the outside world. The booby traps? Yes, they are there alright, but they were put there not to keep you in; it is to keep others out."

Urgut appeared through the doorway, a part eaten sandwich in his hand. He looked at each in turn questioningly, then after a moment's hesitation, "well let's go," he spluttered out through a mouthful of bread.

They started by looking around the homestead. Urgut showed him the rest of the house, the stable, the barn and the implement shed. "I must remember the exact location of things," Mike muttered to himself as he eyed up a pick. Finally they ventured up the hill at the back of the buildings, where he could get a full vista of the valley below. He would have loved to make a sketch, but that would have been far too obvious. His real goal was to commit to memory as much of the terrain as possible so they could traverse it in the dark. Immediately below them lay the homestead, sheds and corrals. Beyond was the small copse of trees, but after that were meadows for hundreds of yards down to the river, and likewise for over 1/2 mile beyond to the foothills on the other side. Looking down the valley he saw the forest. It was a lot larger than he had thought, and he did not think that they had travelled that distance when they had brought him in. This made him more than a little apprehensive as regards the distance he had calculated to the cave. From here though, he could see that the road was basically down this side of the valley, and the river on the other. The exception he knew was near the cave. He remembered that crossing, and it was deep and fast, so he decided that they would cross up this end as soon as possible, and make their way down hugging the cover of the rocks on the valley edge. In front of him here and there were little patches of bush and trees, but to make their escape across in the open, would be futile. They would stand out like a sentinel. Mike cast his eyes up the valley. The same applied there. They could travel up a mile or two, then cross over, unseen in the dark, or they could head back up here behind the homestead, down through the light density trees to the forest. Then they could travel through the forest, crossing the river under the cover of the trees and right across to the other side. That would be the plan, he decided there and then.

"Man oh man this is a beautiful place," he said.

"Yes it truly is," Urgut replied, "I'll miss it even when I'm gone," he added with a catch in his throat.

Mike suddenly felt an immense pity for him, for all of them, and for a moment caught himself starting to feel like a traitor in their midst. Then he thought of Paula, and he knew he must carry on with the deception.

"We've got work to do." Marcus's voice from came from below, and they descended to the corral.

Mike watched as Urgut brought in one of the horses and then attached a wooden sled to the yoke.

"This is Flame," he said matter-of-factly as he tightened up a buckle, "she's a good girl, strong and willing. Ever broken in a horse before?"

"No, but I've ridden a few," Mike replied.

"Then we will have to teach you. For now you can ride Splash." He gave a little giggle. "Splash, we called her that because she loves to splash about in the river, even as a young' un. She gave birth about two years ago and her foal is nearly ready to be broken in. We can go see her later."

"Were the horses always here?"

"Na, they were brought in, and we just keep the breed going."

Mike stood up and wandered around the barn. He noted the locations of rope and tools, things that they might need on their escape.

"That's it," Urgut announced as he did a final check on the halter. He moved forward to in front of the small shed. "This is the tool shed, can you grab that saw over there, the one hanging on the wall; just put it on the sled."

Mike did as he was asked and then followed Urgut out into the sunshine. A light breeze just took the sharpness out of the heat. Little grass bugs and butterflies flitted out of their way as they headed down the track towards the forest. A slight haze of dust occasionally lifted into the air, as a gentle gust of wind blew across the grass filled fields. Birds darted in and out of the waving stems, deftly plucking the insects unfortunate enough to be in sight at that time, and the warbling songs of the many species, along with the rhythmic clip-clop of Flame's hooves serenaded them on their way. Mike breathed deeply. The air was so sweet that he felt he could taste it. He had never noticed that grass had a smell before, and that dust smelt earthy. Horse droppings he decided however, always smell the same. He sidestepped the latter and allowed the peace and tranquillity to soak into his body. The forest was much closer now and he was able to see that it was predominantly podocarp, mainly Rimu and Kahikatea, giving way to Black Beech as the trees climbed up the sides of the mountains. Some broadleaf species, like Tawa interspersed with a variety of others. As they moved in past the tree line the whole experience changed. Now it was much cooler with the sun mostly blocked out, except for the patches of dappled light that forced its way between the clambering trees. The air was full of the moistness of the forest; and the scent of moss and decaying leaves permeated his senses. Mike was however surprised at the openness of the undergrowth. He had expected to find it clogged with vines and bush lawyer, but in the main, ladder fern and tree ferns prevailed, and you could, in places, see a carpet of needles from the towering Rimu trees. They travelled on for about a mile before Urgut led them off to the left up a side trail. About two hundred yards further on they came to a large clearing, across one side of which lay a fallen Kahikatea. Marcus sat comfortably nested in the fork of one of its boughs. He eased himself off the trunk and stretched as they approached. Mike looked over the fallen monster. He estimated that it was some 162 feet in length and at least 5 ft in diameter near the base. Part of the tree had a large limb already cut off and the boys were soon making quick work of the next one. Mike also took turns working the ripsaw, and after two hours they had a sizable stack of roundels to take back to the wood shed. Urgut gently nudged Flame, and she took up the strain on the sled, then they turned and slowly made their way out of the clearing.

CHAPTER 8

It was nearly midday when they arrived back at the house, and as they approached they were greeted by the smell of freshly baked bread. Urgut pulled Flame up beside the woodshed and unhitched the sled, then led her inside to her stable for a feed and well deserved drink. Mike and Marcus had talked about the trees and the bush on the way back, but he saved the one burning question he had until they were all seated at the table, with a generous helping of hot bread and blackberry jam.

"Gran," he asked a bit tentatively, "if the only way into this valley is through the cave, then how did you get all the tools and animals and wagons in, you could not have made them here surely?"

She studied him for a while, trying to assess the motive behind his question, then as though she no longer cared, or maybe because it no longer mattered, replied; "When we first found the caves the entrance was quite large, half the size of this room in fact. There were a few places where we had to pick out a bigger hole on the way through, but we could get a horse and a small wagon in OK. After we found out that we were dead so to speak, we had some dynamite and blew up the entrance to seal it for good."

"Then how did…" The finger rose up again.

"When," she continued, "they put that railway tunnel through, they opened it up again. The railway followed the natural cave for a while, and then when it deviated from the required path, they just bricked up the side passage. When we found out about … about."

"It's OK Gran," Paula interjected.

Gran took a deep breath, "we knew nothing of this until we decided to see it we could find a way out. That's when we found out what they had done. We decided to make use of it and so created our own personal door by removing the bricks in such a way we could put them back to look like it was still solid."

Mike said nothing, and just nodded in understanding.

"Are you coming with us?" Paula asked Gran.

"No dear. I have some sewing to do, and don't worry about making dinner, I'll organise something. You go and enjoy yourself."

"You won't have to. We will have fresh fish," Paula replied as she happily darted off to her room.

After they had cleared away the dishes, they all assembled by the barn. "Do you want to travel up on the dray, or ride bareback," Marcus asked them.

Paula looked at Mike. "I can ride," she stated.

"OK," he replied, "So will I."

Marcus took them into the barn and provided them both with a couple of blankets and a halter made from plaited flax; then he took them down to a small paddock behind the barn. A number of horses grazed contentedly there, but on seeing them approach, they immediately came up to the rail to meet them. Paula gave a little click of her mouth and a piebald mare broke from the bunch and nuzzled her outstretched hand. "This is Terri, short for Teresa." She paused, "It's my mums name," she added quietly. Then a little too quickly "She's my favourite."

Mike thought about his own mother. 'She must be frantic by now. They must be searching for me everywhere. Maybe they will find the cave and rescue ...' his thought stopped short. 'Then they will find this place.' He suddenly realised that he did not want them to find it.

'We have to get out by ourselves' he resolved, 'and no one must find the way in.'

"You can ride Splash again." Marcus's said from behind him."

Mike squeezed through the rails and quietly approached the Mare. Initially she stood back eyeing him up, but soon she relaxed and let him stroke her muzzle. Mike slipped the halter over her nose and flipped the blanket onto her back. He looked around at the others who were also getting ready to mount. He watched as each took their horse to stand by a large rock. Using it as a step they slid onto the horses back, and he, in turn, did the same. It had been a while since he had ridden bare back so it took a few hundred yards before he got anywhere near comfortable. Paula he noted was perfectly at home on a horse and remained close at hand making sure he was not going to fall off. They travelled up the valley, the road at first hugging the bush line to the right, then moving out into the meadows. It was not long before the road and river met about halfway between the valley sides. Mike looked back down behind him, and was surprised at how the valley had narrowed. Before them the river turned across their path and a shallow ford presented itself before them. All the horses walked across normally but Mikes, as soon as she felt the water around her hooves, began to prance. Mike gripped his legs tightly against her flanks expecting her to buck or rear, but instead she just pranced about obviously enjoying herself, kicking up as much water as possible as they crossed. They grouped together on the other side.

"Splash!" stated Mike.

"Yep, that's her," Marcus replied grinning. He looked at Paula, a cheeky grin on her face. Mike just nodded and smiled.

They rode on another one or two miles before he could make out another building on the bush edge to the left. Rounding a small outcrop of rocks the boys stopped and Urgut removed his hat. As Mike came up beside him he saw that it was a small cemetery, consisting of nine graves with white headstones, the words faded but still clearly readable.

"The Richardson's," Urgut said without a prompt from anyone.

"Good people," Marcus added, then turned his horse away and headed up towards the house.

Urgut followed, but Mike sat a while longer looking at the little plot. He turned as Paula moved up beside him.

"They are the last," Paula said almost in a whisper. Mike looked up, following Paula's gaze at the retreating riders. A Tui warbled in the trees above him. He scanned the branches but could not see it. He looked around him at the mountains, at the forest and the river traipsing its way downward through the fields. When he looked back, Paula was watching him.

"It's getting to you, isn't it?" She said at last.

"How do you mean?"

She shrugged. "The valley. Its peace, its presence, it draws you in, it makes you feel so safe."

"Do you really want to leave then?"

The words struck her like a hammer. A flood of emotions swept over her, the first being of anger.

'How dare he!' she thought. After all she'd been through, the kidnapping, the trauma, how dare he suggest that she would not want to leave this beautiful valley.

'This beautiful valley that has been my home all these months.' Suddenly she felt drained. Anger was replaced with a deep sadness. 'Its peace, its presence, it draws you in; it makes you feel so safe. Those are my words,' she conceded to herself.

She returned her gaze to meet Mikes. "I don't know," she replied quietly, "I truly don't know."

"Come on you two," called a distant voice. "Fish are waiting."

Mike looked up to see Urgut standing by the veranda, a fishing pole in his hand. He waved his arm broadly, signalling them to come. He gave Splash a gentle nudge and moved off in Urgut's direction.

Paula held back, stunned by her own admission, then when Mike was halfway to the house, she flicked the reins and slowly followed. He had dreaded asking that question, but a few times she had made comments that made him unsure of her determination to leave. This concerned him, because up till now he had been planning for two. Now he had to consider going it alone, and more worryingly, would she betray him if he did. He slid down off Splash, tied the reins to the hitching rail, and looked around. It was obvious that the house was not lived in, but was still well kept just the same. Not as big as the Kennard's home, it was still laid out much the same. A barn and stables were still in good condition and so was the corral.

"You still maintain this place then?" he asked Urgut.

"Yep, and the Williams place downstream."

"Why?"

"Sentimental I guess, but also for you two," he added. "You can have your choice."

He turned as Paula reined in beside them. She looked pained, and did not meet their eyes.

He was about to say something when a commotion erupted down at the waters edge. He had not noticed Marcus until now, standing half hidden by a clump of Toetoe. He now emerged fighting a fish out in the stream.

He moved down the shingle trying to keep an even tension on the line. Mike noted that he had no reel, so playing the fish was going to be a real challenge. They watch as he worked the rod, allowing it to bend and stiffen, using the suppleness of it. He was constantly moving in and out of the water to tire the fish out. It took a good fifteen minutes, and then there was a lot of splashing in the shallows.

"Come on, get the flippin thing will ya," Marcus yelled at them.

Urgut sprinted down the shingle and into the water. He bent down and scooped up the Giant Kōkopu, carrying it quickly to the shore.

Mike strolled down beside Urgut and eyed the catch. "Nice," he said.

"They are all like this, mostly," he replied grinning excitedly.

Mike nodded but turned his gaze towards the house. Paula sat on the edge of the veranda staring down at the ground, her arms across her knees. He wanted to go to her, but she had to work this out for herself.

Another fish followed, and another, till they had 6 in total lying on the shingle.

"That's enough," Marcus stated, as he rolled up his line, and headed back to the house.

"What's wrong with you?" he asked Paula as he climbed the steps, "You are normally the first to catch a fish."

"I know, a lovers quarrel. You two are going to have to get along sometime."

"Shut up!" She snapped back, "leave me alone all of you." Then grabbing her horse, she mounted and galloped back down the valley.

The three men watched her go in silence. "She was like this when she first came here," Urgut sighed, "real fiery, wouldn't talk."

"Well what did you expect after being abducted," Mike replied looking pointedly at Marcus.

"Oh, in case you wondered; I was serious about the booby traps," then he turned and walked over to his horse. He took a sack from a bag hanging from the saddle and marched down to the fish.

Both had fired a cheap shot, but it did remove any doubt that Mike might have had on the subject of escape. Mike looked back down the trail, but Paula was long gone. 'He knows I'll try, I will have to be very careful,' he thought. 'And I might be attempting this escape on my own.'

"Let's go," Urgut exclaimed as he mounted his steed, "I'm getting hungry," then he turned and trotted off down the valley.

Mike picked up Splashes reigns, and led her to the side of the porch, then carefully climbed on her back and not waiting for Marcus, followed Urgut towards the river.

He found him waiting at the crossing.

"Thought I'd wait in case you needed a hand," he chortled happily.

"Thanks."

They rode on side by side, Urgut telling him about this adventure and that trail, totally at home in his world. 'Irrepressible, that's what he is' smiled Mike to himself. But he was preoccupied with other thoughts. A list of things he would need was foremost on his mind, and where to get them. He still had his day pack and hiking gear, but he would need ropes, and sacks, food for ..., 'How long will it take me to get out? If I take a horse ... no, although much quicker, it would be too burdensome.

Too awkward to hide and too noisy. It will have to be on foot, and at night. So, two maybe three days to the end of the valley, then the caves. Can't use the normal way we came out, they will be watching that, so another way out. That will mean exploring in the dark, so torches for another two days? That's five days. And a spade, and a pick to get out into the tunnel.'

"You can help Urgut fix a few rails on the corral tomorrow." The voice from behind startled him from his thoughts.

"OK," Mike replied. He had not heard Marcus come up from behind, and felt stupidly ashamed that he had been caught planning his escape. 'Idiot,' he chastised himself, 'why am I feeling guilty.'

The smell of burning wood soon played on his nostrils and he knew that they were nearly back. He reigned in at the corral and dismounted, a little gingerly.

"Not used to riding?" Urgut chided from just inside the barn.

"Not bareback," he replied as he rubbed his aching backside.

"I'll take her, if you like."

"Yea, thanks Urgut. I'll just walk around a bit to stretch the kinks out."

Mike looked about for Marcus, but he had already passed his mount onto Urgut and was heading for the house with the bag of fish.

Now was his chance to identify what he thought he might need, and he headed for the tool shed. Quickly he noted the location of a number of items, and then ambled up to the chicken coop. He thought of taking one, but quickly dismissed the idea. It would be far too noisy to get one, and he would then need a fire to cook it, and he didn't want that. 'Damn,' he suddenly realised that he had no idea about food or torches. He had left that up to Paula, but now her companionship was in doubt. In fact, could he even trust her to keep his intent a secret? He felt sure he could, then realised he didn't really have a choice.

Mike slowly made his way back to the house and washed his hands in the outside bowl by the kitchen. He could hear Paula moving about inside. He would have to talk to her about his plans, but maybe not tonight, he dare not risk upsetting her too much considering his current dependence on her help.

Maybe he could talk her into coming if he worked on it for a day or so, that would be the best outcome, but ultimately the choice was still hers. He nodded in confirmation to himself, then slowly made his way over to the garden seat.

CHAPTER 9

The sun had nearly set when he heard Urgut's voice from the porch. "Come and get it."

Mike took one last look out over the valley. A light mist was forming over the river. The birds were singing their evening chorus, and the tops of the trees far up the hill were bathed in a deep orange glow. He could not blame her if she decided to stay. Two years in this paradise, even though she had been abducted. He could only guess the turmoil she must be going through. Even now he knew he would miss the place, but his desire to be back with his family was still much stronger. Rising slowly, he made his way up the steps and opened the door. All were seated in their normal positions; even Paula sat in her chair beside his. They all looked up expectantly, except Paula, waiting for him to sit. On the table was two bowls of steaming vegetables and at each setting a whole fish, steamed and split open with the end hanging over the side of the large platters. Mike took his seat beside her and only then did she glance at him, giving him a quick smile.

"What is wrong dear?" asked Gran. "You have hardly said a thing since you got back, and well ahead of the others."

"It's all right Gran, just that time of month."

"Oh, OK," Gran replied, obviously not convinced by the tone of her voice. "And you?" looking pointedly at Mike.

"Fine Gran. A bit sore in places, that's all." Meeting her look with a smile.

"Hmmm. Marcus if you would."

They all put their heads down. Mike considered moving his hand to take Paula's, but instead put it on the side of his leg, but purposely skimming hers as he did so. A slight smile crossed his lips as he felt her fingers touch his, and he moved his leg so that her hand could fit down into his palm. Marcus finished grace, then they ate, mainly in silence, most feeling a little awkward considering Paula's perceived mood. Mike however, knew that for him at least, the ice was broken, but he made no move to change the mood of the room by tying to engage her in conversation. This was a situation of her making and she could change it if she chose. When they finished, Mike collected the plates and took them to the kitchen, then casually, but purposely, made his way back outside to the bench seat. He had not sat there for long before he wished he had given this a bit more thought. The night air was decidedly cooler and he really wanted to go and get his coat, but he knew as soon as he did, Paula would come out and the chance to talk could be lost for the night, so he pulled his arms in tightly against his body and shivered.

He felt her presence almost before he heard her. Hands gently on his shoulders and then a blanket fell around him. He held up his left arm spreading the blanket for her and she immediately obliged, snuggling in against him. They sat in silence for several minutes before she dropped her bombshell.

"I've set aside food for us for 4 days, and lamps. When are we leaving?" she whispered. The words left him speechless for a few moments. "You didn't think I would stay did you?" she added.

"Well… you did seem a little unsure back there."

She looked up and out across the dark valley, turning it into daylight in her imagination. The fields, flowers, the sunlight dancing off the ripples on the river, and the majestic snow capped mountains beyond, all were burned indelibly on her mind.

"I miss my family, but if you had not come, I would have been happy here. You made me realise just how completely I have accepted my situation, and yes I will be sad to leave this place. But you, you are not that attached, like I was for the first year I suppose, the desire to get back to your loved ones is the only desire." She stopped again. Mike looked at her, sensing that she wanted to say more, but for more than a minute she stared vacantly into the darkness. "If you were staying I would too. But you are going, and seeing you has revived my longing to see my family again. And now I have a new reason to leave also."

He looked at her intently, but she did not return his stare. Mike was not slow on the uptake, but neither was he going to read between the lines. They sat in silence a while longer, then he whispered, "Tonight, just after midnight. I'll be at your window. Make your bed up like you are still asleep in it," he said quietly. Paula nodded, then giving him a swift kiss on the cheek; she quickly rose and walked back inside.

It was about 10pm when they went to bed. Mike lay awake listening, the same as he had the night before. He heard the two doors close. The wait seemed like hours, but was probably only thirty minutes before he heard a shuffling at the window, and saw a shadow darken the room. He had decided that he needed to get the gear he had identified in the barn and tool shed together and stashed somewhere before he got Paula. She had already told him that she was all prepared, but the sudden revelation of her intent had taken him off guard, and he was not really ready for a swift escape. Although the

Kennard's had treated them well under the circumstances, he was not sure of what sort of reaction they might get if they got caught escaping. Someone who sets booby traps could be capable of anything, he reasoned, and he did not want to risk Paula being involved if he did get found getting the tools together. At least then he could protest her innocence and maybe save her from any retribution. Mike rose, and after carefully checking outside the window slipped through and made his way quickly to the tool shed being careful to keep well away from the corral with the horses. There were no doors, so he could see just enough to make out items in the dark. He quickly located a length of rope, and some twine, but could not find the pick he had spied earlier. He was just slipping back out when he laid eyes on an old axe.

"That will have to do," he said to himself and slipped back into the night. A sudden flurry of noise beside him stopped him in his tracks. Then a few coos and gaggles told him he had disturbed the chickens. Hastily he moved behind the shed. One of the horses whinnied.

"Hell, I've done it now" Mike exclaimed under his breath as he quickly made his way around to the other side of the house and down into the trees, out of sight of the lookout. He lifted up some dead branches and hid the rope and axe under them, covering them over with some dead leaves. Mike was almost back at the house when he heard low voices coming his way. He flattened himself against the wall.

"Something disturbed the animals."

"Could be a cow or even a kiwi."

"Could also be them."

"He was in bed a few minutes ago." Mike recognised Urgut's voice.

"Has he moved?" asked the other. Mike guessed it was Marcus.

"Don't know." Urgut replied.

"I might sneak in and check."

Mike's heart sank.

But luckily both moved off around the front. As soon as they were out of sight he sprinted for the window, and slipped in.

Throwing the top blanket back he ripped the others out he had used for stuffing and jumped in fully clothed, boots and all. He only just got the top blanket over himself as he heard the latch open. He lay there motionless, his heart thumping in his chest, then purposely groaned and half turned. A moment later the door shut.

"That was close," he said to himself as he eased out of bed.

Quietly he got all his few clothes together and put them in his pack, then lay back in bed waiting for the Midnight check. After another hour the now familiar shadow appeared in the window then moved on. He waited another five minutes before he got up and made up his bed, to look like he was still in it, then very quietly he slipped out of his window. He did not knock on Paula's window, just gently opened it. She was already waiting with a big sack of goods and her pack. He quickly checked that her bed looked good enough to fool them for a while, then they both slipped out, past the outside toilet, and into the night.

"Wait here," Mike whispered and disappeared.

Paula stood huddled against a tree, her heart pounding. She nearly screamed as Mike suddenly was beside her again.

"We need to get up into the tree line above us and skirt around the homestead, then down to the forest. Urgut will be sitting on the seat we used tonight," he whispered.

"Follow me," Paula said quietly but commandingly in his ear, and she moved off up the hill behind the barn. Some men might have been miffed by her sudden leadership role, but Mike did not argue. She knew this place far better than he did, so he obediently followed. She did not go straight as Mike had anticipated, but slipped away up the valley for about 100 yards, then made their way up. Mike followed unquestioningly, until they were well clear of the homestead and moving along a small path the headed down towards the forest.

"Why the detour?" he asked as he moved up beside her.

"Didn't want to disturb the chickens," she replied softly, "they can make quite a racket."

'Don't I know it,' he said to himself, but out loud, "I'm glad you're with me, I would have ploughed straight into the wire."

They moved on together as quickly and as silently as they could, until they were above the house and could get a good view of the surrounding area, there they sat down and got their breath.

"What time do you think it is?" whispered Paula.

Mike stood up and slowly turned around. "Twenty past one."

He looked down at Paula who was staring at him incredulously.

He returned his gaze to the star filled night.

"Twenty past one", he stated confidently.

"I'm impressed, will you show me how to do that?" Paula asked, following his gaze into the sky, trying to pinpoint what stars one would use to work out the time.

"Sure," he replied and pulling his hand out of his coat, and held a pocket watch in front of her face.

She slowly lowered her head, shaking it. Mike had not joked with her like this before and he wondered how she would respond. He sat back down on his haunches and gave her a furtive look. The response was immediate. A sudden sideways shove left him sprawled on the ground. He looked into her face, and he could tell she was trying very hard not to burst into laughter.

"One up to you," she said grinning.

Mike knew at that moment a very special bond was forming between them. One formed out of adversity and a need to have someone to believe in, to trust in. He knew at that their friendship would be for life, but he sensed something more developing between them, something he had never contemplated before, could …

"The moon is just coming up, follow me." Her words broke him out of his thoughts.

Picking up his pack and checking he still had the tools, he followed her towards the tall trees that loomed in front of them. 'Just maybe,' he smiled to himself.

"Do you think we should risk making our way down the edge of the tree line," Paula asked quietly.

"No, we need to move up the road edge still in the cover of the trees before we cross the road, you can see quite a way in from the house."

She nodded and they moved forward until they were about 50 yards from the road, then they turned left and still keeping well clear of any open spaces, moved further down the valley.

They had travelled about a mile when Paula stopped. "There is a trail on the other side that leads down to the river if we cross here," she said.

Mike carefully moved to the road edge and looked back towards the homestead. He listened intently but heard nothing but the gentle rustle of the breeze in the trees. Paula slipped up beside him. "OK let's go quickly," Mike decided.

They darted out from the trees and across the road; stopped just inside the tree line; and waited. Nothing. Paula tapped him on the arm, and indicated that he should follow. He nodded, and they disappeared into the trees. Even though they were following a trail, out of the light of the moon, the path was very difficult to keep to. Many times they took a wrong turn, only to find themselves in a tangle of vines. Having to backtrack was time consuming and Mike was getting worried that they may not make the protection of the far side of the valley before light. They pressed on in silence. The noise of their progress, which even though they were being careful, sounded to Mike like a herd of elephants trampling a corrugated iron shed.

Paula suddenly stopped dead, and Mike nearly pushed her over as he crashed into her.

"Listen!" she whispered urgently.

This time he heard it too.

A crash in the bushes about twenty yards to the right of them.

They froze, hearts pounding in their chests.

Again, closer this time.

Mike looked around for a way to escape. How far could they run? Ten yards; twenty maybe before they got tangled in the trees; he looked back at the approaching noise and awaited their fate. Paula clutched him tightly as the bushes parted not more that 2 yards away and there stood a very startled cow. They all stared at each other for several seconds, then the cow spun to his left and crashed off into the night.

Paula didn't know whether to laugh or cry.

She didn't have time to do either before this time Mike suddenly put up his hand to silence her.

"Listen."

Paula sucked in her breath expecting the worst.

"No listen," whispered Mike. "I can hear the river."

"Yes so can I," Paula said as she breathed out, her heart still pounding.

It still took them nearly thirty minutes to reach its banks. They stayed just inside the tree line looking for any sign of movement.

"Do you think we can cross here?" asked Mike.

"I don't think so, it's very rocky, but down further there is a swimming hole and just below that there is a shingle bar, we can cross there."

"OK let's go."

Again they moved off keeping just inside the tree line. It was much easier walking here with only a few ferns and small bushes to impede their progress. As they walked they could easily hear the bubbling of the water as it rushed amongst the rocks, but almost suddenly the sound stopped.

"Swimming hole," stated Paula, and then moved a little further down stream where they could hear the gentle babble of water over small stones. "We'll cross here," she added.

"Let's try and keep our feet below the surface, and drag our legs through the water to keep the noise down," Mike suggested.

They moved through the ankle to knee-deep water, careful not to break the surface with a splash. The river was wider than Mike had guessed and he was pleased with her decision to cross here, rather than wait till later when the water would most likely be much faster and deeper. They entered the cover of the forest, still heading for the now much closer mountains. This time there was no track, and they just had to push their way through the tangle of vines and bush. It was not long however before the land began to rise. They reached a bush flat and sat down in a little clearing exhausted.

"How much further?" Paula asked.

Mike looked up at the sky. He thought he could see a slight lightening to the east.

"The East, of course, you idiot." Mike suddenly exclaimed standing up and looking around. "Now I can orientate the valley with the outside world."

"East … its over that way," Paula replied matter-of-factly, indicating over her shoulder. "You only had to ask."

Mike sighed, "I only had to ask." He looked down at her now dirty, pretty face. 'I really like this girl,' he thought. The realization suddenly struck him, he could see her face.

"Let's get going a bit further. I want to try and get high enough to be able to see across to the homestead, before they realise we have gone. Then we may be able to see what action they will take."

Again they scrambled on. The ground was much steeper now, and there were rock formations to move around. Suddenly it got much brighter for two reasons. Firstly, dawn had come, and secondly they were at the top of a small knoll.

"Let's get up behind that outcrop of rocks," Mike said.

Carefully they made their way up, making sure they were not in sight, and crawled to the top on their stomachs. Before them lay the valley. A light mist covered the river and lower meadows. The early morning sun was some way from topping the mountains, so the whole vista was bathed in a soft pale light. It was magnificent.

"This place is so beautiful," she said without looking at him.

"Yes it is," he replied.

"Look… at the homestead, I guess they know we are gone."

Mike looked. Someone was hitching up a horse to the two-wheeled cart. Silently they watched as they climbed on and trotted down the drive to the road and towards the forest.

"The question is," whispered Mike, "are they good enough to track us? If so we have to keep moving, if not, then maybe they will just wander around looking to find us. I guess we are about to find out," he added as the cart entered the forest.

In his mind he followed the cart, although unseen, through the trees, and tried to project when it would come out; provided they had not found their trail and were tracking.

"About now," he said.

Nothing. They waited another 10 minutes, then just as his heart began to sink; the cart appeared and continued down the valley. He watched for a while as it travelled down the road at a normal trot.

Strange, thought Mike not being able to put his finger on exactly why.

Paula nudged him. "Look," she said, indicating in the direction of the homestead again.

Another horse was being hitched, this time to the four-wheeled wagon. They saw another figure loading something in the back. No one appeared to be in a hurry.

"Do they realise we have gone?" asked Paula, "or do they think we have just gone for a walk?"

"Oh they know we have gone. They would have found our beds made up to look like we were still there. They know we are on foot, and they have horses," replied Mike.

"There is another alternative, that we, or at least I have not thought of," Paula said with a sort of hopelessness in her voice, that brought Mike swiftly around to look at her. He tilted his head quizzically.

"There is only one way out. They can sit at the entrance of the cave and just wait for us."

Mike slid down from the top of the rock and propped himself up with his back against it. Paula joined him. They sat in thought for a while, contemplating the situation.

"You're a smart girl," Mike said at last. "I hadn't considered that one at all either, and judging by their behaviour, I'm sure you are right. They know we have limited food and resources, and they have all the time in the world. They just need to block our escape and wait for us to either starve or give ourselves up."

Paula cuddled his arm. "There's no hope for us then," she said sadly.

Mike looked at her. "For us there is every hope."

She hugged him tighter.

"But as for escape … well I'm not ready to give up just yet, but for now, let's get over there in the cover of those bushes and get some rest, we have a long way to go."

Paula gave his hand a squeeze, and followed him. They made a quick bed out of ferns. Paula pulled a large blanket from the pack she carried, laid it out, half covering the ferns, and they lay down. She reached back and flicked the other half over both of them then snuggled in against him. Both were asleep in seconds.

CHAPTER 10

Mike woke with the sun streaming on his face. He gave a little start as he realised that Paula was not beside him, then, as he raised himself he saw her sitting a few feet away on a rock.

"Breakfast?" She asked, moving over to sit beside him, offering a cheese and tomato sandwich.

He suddenly realised that he had forgotten to tell her not to light any fires, then just as quickly realised that he did not have to. This girl was no fool. Can you fall in love with someone in just 2 days? He mused.

"Thanks," he said taking it from her.

They ate in silence, then bending down, she picked up a cup of water and passed it to him.

"At least we won't die of thirst," Mike said mostly to himself.

"We won't die at all," Paula quickly added, looking intently at him.

Mike smiled at her. "I will if I sit here much longer," he said as he stood up rubbing his backside and stretching.

"What are you going to do when we get out?" he suddenly asked, surprising himself at his own question.

"Go and see Mom and Dad, they must have given me up for dead long ago."

"Me too," Mike replied. "ahhh …anyone else?"

"Like who?"

"Ahhh …your husband, or boyfriend maybe?" he asked awkwardly.

Paula smiled. "Fishing are we?"

Mike stared at his feet, his face starting to glow. He suspected that she might be enjoying this.

"It's all right, there is no-one else in my life." She paused "But what about you?"

Mike breathed a quiet sigh of relief, but also thought that he might have detected a slight concern in her voice, maybe a realization that she had not considered before?

"Likewise," he said.

They packed up the blanket and food in silence, and then climbed back up the rock to check on what was happening, both slightly embarrassed at the exchange, but both now secretly happy it had been dealt with, and with mutually pleasing results. The road was clear, no sign of any movement. They could see someone moving around the homestead though. They appeared to be hanging out washing.

"She's too old to be doing that," Paula said in disgust, "I should be ..." her voice trailed off and she looked down at the ground. Mike just put his arm around her shoulder and gave her a hug. "Let's go," she said decisively, and slid back down off the rock.

They made their way down the valley keeping to the outcrops and bushes as much as possible, always watching for any sign of movement on the plain below. The terrain this far up the side of the valley was fairly easy to move through. They were about 500 yards up from the valley floor. Here Beech trees tended to keep the forest carpeted with a layer of small leaves, and the underbrush was sparse, comprising mainly of fern, and low pittosporums. This band of trees was about 200 yards wide. Higher than that, the vegetation was less as it became steeper and rocky, with more open places, but even at that height movement could attract unwanted attention. Below this band, the bush became much more lush, and therefore denser. Here was the podocarp forest, consisting mainly of Rimu and Totara. Vines hung from the trees, and a large variety of ferns and bushy plants made travel slow and noisy.

They were moving down the valley so one would have thought that as it widened out the going would be easier. Technically it was, but with the wider valley came more ridges and spurs that encroached out from the main valley's walls, and these created their own problems. The decision had to be made whether to go around them or over them. A wrong decision would mean having to back track and that all took time. The other issue was vision. Mike wanted to keep a reasonable eye on what was happening out over the valley, but to do this they need to be high enough to see over those majestic Totaras, and again this meant either moving further away to gain enough height, or moving just inside the bush line. But for now everything was just right, well almost.

Mike looked up. For the first time since he had been there, clouds now sailed across the once clear sky. Initially they had just been white fluffy cotton balls, now however they had a much greyer shade and were starting to bank up. By midday he could see a definite front moving in. "I guess it must rain in paradise also," he said as they sat down on a ledge to rest.

"It has its moments, snows in winter too," Paula replied.

"We had better stop well before dark and find some shelter for tonight."

Paula looked around. "I think there is a rocky outcrop or cave a bit further on, around that next headland. I have seen it from the river once or twice when I have been out riding."

"Great we will make for that then."

Mike stood up and looked out across the valley through the branches of a small conifer. Paula was halfway up when his hand dropped firmly on her shoulder.

"Stand up very slowly," he said.

She did as she was told and scanned across the river. At first she saw nothing, then, just on the other side a rider appeared from behind some bushes and walked his horse slowly along the river edge.

"Do you think he has seen us?" she whispered.

"No I don't think so. We are still fairly well concealed, and I think he is concentrating more on looking for our tracks, rather than for us directly. But it does tell us two things."

Paula looked across at him, but he did not shift his gaze.

"One is that they are actively looking, and two is that they have no idea where we are. I think that they probably guessed it that we would take the fastest most direct route down the valley, instead of up here in the bush."

"But why bother, I mean as long as they have the cave covered, why look?"

"Human nature I guess. There is nothing worse that just sitting and waiting for something to happen. I would think that they take turns guarding the cave while the other goes out looking. It is something to do."

"You know a fair bit about human nature don't you?"

Mike looked at her and smiled. "Something you pick up when working with animals I guess. Horses, cows, sheep, dogs, cats, humans; all can communicate without words. You just need to read and understand their body language. The way they use their eyes, ears and sounds, it's all about understanding their basic instincts and behaviours. Most people just don't bother to listen."

Paula looked him straight in the eye. It was a communication they both understood. She gave her nose a little wrinkle and hugged him.

"Let's get moving," he said.

It was about 3pm when they stopped. Mike estimated that they had travelled about 2 miles. Not much distance but they were being careful not to raise any dust or dislodge any rocks that would attract attention. They sat under the branches of a large beech tree, and had a meal of fruit and cheese. The valley was starting to close in a bit. The terrain getting steeper, and the river was now almost directly below them hugging the foot of the hills, and although the road was still about a mile distant the risk of being seen by someone was getting greater. After checking that the coast was clear, they started off again, but had only gone about 50 yards when Mike suddenly stopped. As Paula came up beside him she could see why. They were standing on the edge of a sheer drop of nearly 50 feet straight down.

"I'm glad we didn't find that in the dark," Paula remarked.

"So am I, I think we had better only move in daylight from now on," Mike replied.

"How are we going to get around it?"

Mike looked across the gap. 'Not that way,' he thought.

"Either up or down I guess," he said.

"I don't like heights, so down," Paula answered quickly.

"OK, down it is, but we are going to have to back track a bit until we find a way. About a couple of hundred yards back, I think I saw a path going down."

They retraced their steps to the place where an animal track headed off down the side of the hill. It was steep, but walkable with care. The only problem was that they would be totally exposed to anyone watching from the other side.

A crash of thunder echoed down the valley.

Mike considered their options. If they went down now, and anyone came along the road, they would very likely be seen. If they waited till dark, it would be too dangerous. A few drops of rain hit him in the face. He looked back up the valley at the advancing downpour. "If we time this right we might be OK. If we go as the rain hits, it will obscure us from the road, and we will still be able to see. But if we wait too long, this slope could become too slippery to negotiate. What do you think?"

Paula thought for a moment. "Let's do it!" she said opening her pack and pulling out her jacket.

Five minutes was all it took for the rain to become a steady downpour. Mike looked out over the valley and saw nothing but a grey swirling mist. "If we can't see the road they can't see us" Paula gave him a decisive nod, and they started down the slope, Mike in the lead.

The descent was less of a problem than they thought. Many tree roots and rock outcrops provided them numerous hand and foot holds, and although they had the odd slip, they arrived at the bottom fairly much intact, with only a few bits of skin left on the rough rock surfaces. By now however, the rain was bringing on a premature nightfall, and Mike was very much aware that they needed protection from the elements.

"I didn't think it ever rained here," he said gloomily.

"Sorry my darling, but the valley needs rain to survive just like on the outside."

He looked back at her, surprised by her words. She caught his look and looked down shyly, giving her nose that cute little wrinkle, but said nothing more.

It was dark when they reached the river only a few yards to their left, but they had heard its roar before they saw it. Mike put his mouth up to her ear. "We have to find that shelter, let's make our way down the side of the river."

The ground here was quite swampy and they made slow progress pushing their way through a tangle of vines hanging from the trees and ferns covering the spongy ground. Small streams of water began to cross their path. Moss and fungus covered the logs, and they slipped over many times. He pulled his jacket tighter about him as a trickle of water found its way down his neck, and every tree they touched brought a cascade of additional drops down on them. They stopped and took a short rest under a fallen Rimu.

"Are you alright?" he asked her worriedly.

"I'm fine," she said and smiled back at him, but he saw the strain in her face, and put his arm around her pulling her close trying to give some comfort. They waited for a few more minutes hoping that the rain might ease, but if anything it got harder. Mike gave her a nudge, then leaving the comparative dryness of the tree, they pressed on through the storm.

It was about fifteen minutes later when Mike started to hear it. Almost imperceptible at first above the noise of the river, was another sound. Not dissimilar, like two bands playing the same piece of music on opposite sides of a rugby field. At first they sound almost the same, but the closer you get the more you realise that one is playing louder, and in a slightly different key. So it was that they approached a side creek. Normally a pretty trickling stream, now it was a dark threatening torrent.

Mike looked at Paula. Her face drenched with water and smeared with mud. Pieces of fern and twigs clung to her tossed and saturated hair. She looked so tired and vulnerable. "What do we do now?" She still managed a strained smile.

Love can make you do stupid things he thought later, and his next decision was one of them. His desire to protect her from the elements, to get her shelter and warmth clouded his judgment. There were many things he should, would have done, if he had been alone or with a tramping party. He looked again into that beautiful frightened and trusting face, "I'll go across first," he said, and inched his way into the swirling water. Large rocks blocked his every step and he had to slide his feet around each one, balancing against the current until he could get a foothold. He dragged his foot over each obstacle and placed it down firmly, before he negotiated the next rock. The stream was only about 3 yards wide but it took all his time to get across without falling over. Once there he turned around and took two steps back into the water.

"OK, come on across carefully and grab my hand," he called out to Paula.

Carefully she made her way into the current. All was going well until she was just over half way. Suddenly her foot slipped from under her. She threw herself forward grabbing for Mikes hand, their fingers touched, then with a cry and a splash, she disappeared into the darkness.

"Paula, Paula," screamed Mike now unconcerned as to who might hear him.

"Mike help," he heard her splutter through the noise of the river. He rushed down the stream. "Help," he heard again, but this time from almost behind him. He spun around looking for her, then realised that she had been swept out into the main river.

"Paula," he screamed again at the top of his lungs. He thought he heard her call in the distance somewhere downstream; then she was gone.

CHAPTER 11

Vines and twigs ripped at his face and arms as he bolted headlong through the bush beside the river. At every opening he waded out and called, but heard nothing.

He had travelled several hundred yards when, as he waded out again, this time something caught his eye. About 10 yards down from him in an eddy floated Paula's pack.

"No, No, No," he cried as he ploughed towards it through the waist deep water. He reached out to pull her lifeless body to him, and found only a pack. Frantically he scanned around him but saw nothing else. Panic and hope welled up equally inside him as he pulled the pack to shore and pushed on through the undergrowth. He was now at the headland and a small gravel area now gave him faster access along the bush edge. He looked out to the tip of the point he saw an object moving around in the shallower water.

"Paula," he yelled as he ran forward, but he soon realised that it was the food bag. Again his heart sank as he pulled it up on the rocks. Hope was fading fast for him. An incredible weight now fell on his shoulders and he sank to the ground in total despair.

"Mike," the call was very weak.

He jumped to his feet. "Paula, Paula," he screamed at the top of his voice already running along the shingle.

Then he saw her. She was hanging on to the branches of a fallen tree 20 feet from the shore.

"Mike help, help," she called.

"Paula."

"Over here, I can't hang on much longer," she cried spluttering, her body buffeted by the swirling current that threatening to tear her from her handhold. Quickly he took the coil of rope from his arm and tied a knot in the end.

"I will throw the rope out to you, as the water sweeps it down to you, grab hold and I'll pull you in."

He threw the rope out but it fell short.

"I'll try again."

"Hurry, my hands are slipping."

This time it fell far enough out in the water for it to be dragged down towards her. As it touched her she grabbed hold and was immediately swept downstream. Mike hauled on the rope, then there was a lot of splashing in the dark several yards down from him. He ran towards the sound and found her staggering to her feet in the shallows. She fell into his outstretched arms and burst into tears. "I thought I was going to drown," she sobbed. Mike held her trembling body close to him. "I thought I was going to lose you too", he said, tears streaming down his face.

They stood hugging each other for nearly five minutes in the pouring rain neither wanting to let the other go. Finally after Mike felt her stop trembling a little, he led her to a log at the edge of the bush. "Let's find some shelter."

Paula nodded, still unable or unwilling to let go of him. "Stay here and rest. I'll be back in minute or two."

He walked the few yards to where the food bag was and brought to over to her.

"I have your pack too. I'll go and get it."

"I had to get it off, it was pulling me down"

He thought of telling her of the fright he had in seeing it, but just said "Be back shortly."

He quickly retraced his steps and retrieved the pack, then quickly returned to where he left Paula, his spirits renewed.

"I've found the pa ..." he stopped as he surveyed the scene.

Paula sat on the ground sobbing, the contents of the bag strewn around, a pile of soggy mush that was once a loaf of bread in her hands. On seeing him she burst into tears. "I'm sorry, so sorry, it's all ruined," she cried.

Mike went up and kneeling beside her, took her in his arms.

"It's all right sweetheart, it's all right, it's only the bread; all the other food will be just fine."

She clung to him for minutes sobbing, then sitting back and wiping her dirty face, looked up at him. "Thank you for finding me, for saving me."

Mike smiled at her, picked up the food, and put it back in the bag. He then retrieved the blanket, rope and axe, and led her to the safety of the bush line. He improvised a shelter using some branches from a fallen tree, covering them in fern fronds. He then collected dry bracken, and made a bed to insulate Paula from the ground. He retrieved a flint in his backpack and started to gather some tinder so they could start a fire, but Paula insisted that he didn't. "I've come this far, and I'm not going to risk capture for the sake of a stupid fire," she stated defiantly.

Mike reluctantly conceded, but he knew he would need to keep a close eye on her. They huddled together all night, neither getting much, if any sleep. He could feel Paula shivering against him, and that was good. He knew that if she stopped shivering, she could be deteriorating; then he would light a fire. "I'd rather be captured and have you alive, than to lose you for good." She looked up at him, and he stared back staunchly. Paula just nodded.

By dawn the rain had stopped and the sunrise bathed the whole valley in its normal golden glow.

"We need something to eat, and then we need to get dry," Mike said quietly. Paula smiled weakly. She had not yet got over the nights ordeal and Mike was now worried that shock would set in and hypothermia would soon follow. They made their way out onto the shingle bar to catch the early sun. He prepared a meal of cheese and fruit.

"Where do you think that cave is?" he asked.

Paula looked around trying to get her bearings.

"Up there I think." She said pointing to an area of rocks about 200 yards up the side of the hill.

"OK, you get back into the shelter of the bush and I will check it out."

"I can follow you up," she objected.

"NO!" he replied emphatically. "If we are wrong and I have to try another and another path, you will be too exhausted to get there at all. You wait here!"

Mike expected a tirade of objections. Instead she just kissed him on the cheek and sat back down in the shelter. He scouted around the bank for about 150 yards before he found a trail that seemed to lead up to a sheltered rock formation. He scrambled up, but it soon petered out to nothing. Disappointed he retraced his steps. Almost at the bottom he noticed another sidetrack and turned up that. He had gone only 10 yards when it opened up into clear path. Thirty minutes later he was standing on flat area, rocks and shrubs protecting him from view from below, but also affording an excellent view for him over the valley. Behind him was a fairly substantial open shelter. It was a perfect location. Plenty of area to dry things out, and a view over the valley from over the rocks, and not too hard for Paula to get up here, he thought. Pleased with his find, Mike quickly descended to the river flat, and into the bush to find Paula.

As he approached her however, his joy of finding the shelter quickly faded into deep concern. She looked grey and distant.

"What's wrong?" he asked softly kneeling beside her and taking her hand. It was weak and cold.

From the moment they had first met, he had perceived her as a strong woman. Strong in build and in mind, now she looked so fragile and helpless; it both shocked and scared Mike.

"I'm so cold," she whispered feebly. Mike knew he had to get her warm and dry quickly, but now he doubted that she would make it up to the shelter.

"Did you find it?"

"Yes."

"Then let's go." She managed a smile and struggled to her feet. Mike grabbed her as she pitched forward into his arms. "I'm so tired."

Mike knew she had to move, and now. He had to get her muscles moving, to create some inner heat. Tiredness was a major sign that hypothermia was setting in, and although he wanted her to be comfortable, he knew he must not let her succumb. He carefully lifted her to her feet and started to walk her around, getting circulation moving again, then once she was able to stand without help, he picked up her pack and his and the tools. "Give me that," she said as he struggled with the food bag. Mike was about to object, but a renewed strength showed in her eyes. He knew her well enough now, that to imply weakness by objecting would hurt her dignity, so he passed it across. Mike guided her in front of him up the path, staying close behind her to support her on the odd occasion she began to stumble. At first the going was slow. Just a few paces and she stopped for a rest, but by the time they reached the shelter she was almost back to her usual self. Paula emptied her pack, and Mike helped her wring out her sodden clothes and blankets.

Then after checking the valley for any sign of movement, he lay on a patch of low grass behind some low rocks where he would not be seen from below and then took off his wet shirt. He was just about to remove his trousers when he remembered Paula.

"Sorry," he said as he turned back towards her, "I'll give you some privacy."

"Do you have any spare dry clothes, everything of mine is soaked?"

"No, I only came with a daypack," he replied, but started looking through it anyway.

"Oh well, never mind," she replied.

When he turned back towards her, she was stripped to her tattered bra and pants. He looked at her for a moment, and then turned away embarrassed, aware that he had been staring. 'Wow she's beautiful, even when she is totally dishevelled' he thought. He heard her come up beside him.

"Mike!"

"Yep," he replied looking at the ground.

She squatted down and touched him on the arm. "Mike," she said more emphatically this time.

He half turned, making sure he looked her squarely in the eyes.

"I trust you with my life, and I know I can trust you with my chastity also. Now get your wet trousers off, because if you stay in them, by tomorrow you will be the sick one." She picked up his jacket and turned it inside out feeling the lining. "This will do, we need to get out of the wind. That shelter has a dry sandy floor, let's go inside."

He knew she was right. Mike complied, followed her into the shelter, and sat down beside her.

She pushed him back twisting him on his side facing him away from her and laid the jacket over his back between them, then facing the same way snuggled in against him. He felt her breath on his ear. "No man has ever seen me like this, and no other ever will," she whispered, and then gently kissing the edge of his ear, she lay back and drifted off to sleep.

Mike lay there his heart racing and his emotions in turmoil. He was a man of integrity and morals, but he was also grateful at Paula's insight by putting the jacket between them, after all, he was still a man. He thought about what she had said. He went over in his mind the last few hours. From a feeling of total unbelievable loss and despair, to a feeling of...

He thought for a moment. What was he feeling? He had been taken aback and incredibly moved at her total confidence in him. She obviously realised her vulnerability, and yet had placed complete trust in him. A trust he knew he would never betray. He also realised just how incredibly comfortable he was around her. He had been around girls before, but whereas with the others he had felt awkward and uneasy, Paula was so different. It was like he had known her all his life. It was like his life started only a couple of days ago. Mike sucked his breath in deeply. 'Couple.' Her words came flooding back, and he suddenly understood. "No other ever will!" For the first time in his life, he knew how it felt to be unconditionally in love. He wanted to jump, and shout, and hug her, and kiss her; but he just smiled and drifted off to sleep listening to her rhythmic breathing close behind him.

It was after midday when he awoke and gently eased himself from under her arm. He looked down at her. "I love you," he said to himself quietly. He tried to imagine her in a frilly dress, with makeup and perfume, and found it foreign. Instead he just looked at her dirty face, scratched arms and matted hair, and said again "I do love you."

He slipped quietly out of the shelter, shielding his eyes from the bright sunshine. The smell of the native orchids wafted up from below and birds sang their many songs from every tree. Flashes of light reflected off the water, dancing over the river. Wild flowers of every colour and hue swayed over the meadows in the warm gentle breeze. Mike looked to his side at their clothes laid out on the rocks, the only sign of the hellish night that they had endured, and realised just how fragile paradise can be.

A sound echoed up from the valley and Mike peered over the top of their rock fortress. Movement caught his eye. It was the horse and dray heading back to the homestead. He looked intently.

Paula crawled up beside him. Almost unthinkingly he put his arm around her and kissed her on the cheek. She turned her head and looked at him quizzically. Their eyes met. He smiled at her, and then he returned his gaze to the valley. In that instant she new something between them had changed. She looked out across at the distant figure and smiled also. Then casting her eyes skyward "Thank you," she said quietly.

"Only one on it, so the other must still be at the cave." His words broke into her thoughts. "If it stays dry tonight," he scanned the almost cloudless sky, "and they are making daily trips to the cave, we should be able to follow where they are going, and see its location. We must keep a regular watch to make sure we don't miss their return trip."

"Great idea," she replied

By 2 o'clock they had all dried out and were dressed again. The blanket however would need a lot more time, but they had to move on. After a quick meal of cheese and nuts, Mike led them back down to the river flat. Down here they could move much quicker, but had little view over the valley.

It was about 6 pm when they again heard the rattle of horse and cart in the distance. Mike quickly darted up a little slope, and watched from behind a bush. The cart travelled down the valley and out of sight behind a spur. He watched for a while longer, but saw no further sign.

He descended to Paula.

"We are not far enough down to work out where they are going, maybe tomorrow. Let's find a bed for the night before it gets too dark."

He scanned the hills and soon spotted an outcrop of rock not too far up the hill, and about another 400 yards downstream. This time they gathered some bracken fern and made a comfortable mattress. Paula spread out the damp blanket, and then decided that they would just use it as a top cover if they needed it.

"I wish we could have a fire," she said as she cuddled up to him.

"So do I. We could spear some fish and have a hot meal. I saw some in the river today."

Removing a comb from her pack, she valiantly attempted to comb her matted hair.

"I wish I could have a hot bath to. I must look an absolute mess."

He looked at her and smiled. "You look just fine." And he meant it. "I don't look to hot myself," he added as he rubbed the growing beard on his chin.

"There is not much left to eat, only a few apples and pears, a handful of nuts each, and a chunk of slightly mouldy cheese."

"We must be close to the cave by now, so we need food for tomorrow, but we will need a couple of days worth while we are inside. I will see if I can find something in the morning, it will be our last chance. There must be some fruit or berries around here somewhere," Mike replied.

Paula gave him a sharp look. "Don't eat ANY berries, without me checking them first."

"Hell I hadn't thought about that," he said suddenly remembering that the boys were infertile.

"You haven't eaten any have you?" Paula asked anxiously.

"No"

"Good, I would like to have kids …" She suddenly stopped what she was doing, and gave him a nervous glance, realising what she had just said. Mike was looking directly at her.

"So would I," he casually replied.

She wrinkled her nose shyly and carried on with preparing a meagre meal. They sat eating quietly, and watched as the sun slowly vacated the valley, leaving only a soft light, then that too faded into darkness.

Paula started as a wood pigeon suddenly flew noisily past not two yards from them. She was still a little shaken by the previous nights experience, and cuddled in close against him. He put his arm around her, and lay back against the sloping dirt bank at the rear of the shelter.

Paula put her head on his chest and whispered to herself "I love you."

Mike ran his fingers through her hair. "I love you," he whispered to himself.

CHAPTER 12

The warmth of the sun on his feet is what woke him.

He carefully disentangled himself from Paula's arms and stretched his aching body.

'I am so looking forward to a real bed again' he thought as he surveyed the valley. He pulled out his pocket watch and looked at it, tracing the embossed head of a dog on the cover with his thumb, then he flipped open the lid. Inside was an inscription.

"To Mike on your 21st Love Mum & Dad."

The dog was a Golden Retriever. He had been given it when he was five, and it had died when he was nineteen. Devastated by the loss he had refused another dog, so his parents had the watch especially made for him. He suddenly realised how much he missed them. He coughed back a lump in his throat. "I'll be back with you soon," he said quietly.

Seven thirty he noted, and carefully wound it as he had done every morning.

He felt her hand slide along his arm, cradling it in hers, and then she gently rested her head on his shoulder. Mike was surprised at how natural it felt, like they had been doing it for years. Yet only six days ago he would have been most uncomfortable at the closeness.

"I think today is the day," he finally said.

He knew that they must be only a few hours from the cave, but they still had to locate it, and now they also needed food. They packed up their belongings and Mike led them back down to the river flat, then after a quick wash in the brisk waters, started their trek back down the valley.

A bush-covered promontory now stood before them.

"Do we go around, or over?" Paula asked.

"Over I think."

Another hour and they were standing on top of a narrow ridge. In front of them the valley spread out into a wide plain, but at the bottom end it turned left as the mountains curled around in a huge dogleg.

Mike stopped. "Let's just sit here a while."

"Why?"

"I think we are closer than I estimated. See that small stream over there?" he pointed out across the valley floor. "Well I think that is the little brook I remember being taken across. If I am right then the road will come directly towards us. It should cross the main river down below this ridge. If so, then the cave is up on that cliff facing us."

"Let's go over there and see."

"No let's not be too hasty. If we can see that ridge, I bet someone is sitting there right now looking across at us. They won't be able to see us in this bush, but if we go down there now, we would be seen immediately. Let's move back up the slope a bit so we can get a better view and settle in."

Carefully they made their way up through the bush until they came to the top of a slip that afforded them a clear view of the valley and the mountains. They made themselves comfortable just inside the bush line and waited.

"How are we going to get past them into the cave?" Paula asked.

"I've been thinking about that. How much can you remember about your walk through them after they abducted you?"

"I'm not sure. We went through a lot of caverns, some quite big, and we wound through passages, and even the boys went the wrong way once. We were in there for hours."

"This is a bit of a long shot, but did you notice if at any time there may have been signs of another entrance?"

"Like what for instance?"

"I don't really know, maybe wind in your face from another passage, or…"

"Yes, at one stage as we passed a passage one of the torches nearly blew out." Paula cut in.

"Was it near the entrance or deeper in?"

"Just over halfway I think. I know it was not too near the entrance."

"I thought I felt a breeze from one of the side tunnels too. Was it on your left or right?"

"Left," she replied.

Mike nodded. "Hopefully then somewhere between us and the main cave is another entrance. All we have to do is find it."

It was Paula who saw it first. She nudged Mike and pointed out across the flat. "Here he comes." A little trail of dust had appeared in the distance.

They watched as it approached the stream glistening in the midday sun.

"Yes," Mike exclaimed as it turned towards them. "He should cross about now," he said after a few minutes.

"Well done. Just as you predicted," Paula said happily.

"Now we just need to hope we can locate the cave entrance. That will give us a starting point."

They watched together. Paula snuggled in against him, as they traced the path of the cart as it headed towards the river. Then suddenly it disappeared. Mike sat up straight. "Where did it go?"

"There!" said Paula as it reappeared climbing up a hidden bank on what must have been the far side of the river.

"That's a lot further down than I would have thought. I think I can see the track angling up the side," Mike added.

Sure enough the cart started to ascend the track. It climbed steadily as the rock face got steeper and then about half way up stopped on a ledge. They watched as a figure got off and then he and the cart disappeared behind a rock. Moments later another tiny figure appeared on the ledge, looking out.

"That's it. That's the cave. We can't see it because it faces slightly away from us and is hidden by that rock outcrop. But that is definitely the cave," he said excitedly, and gave Paula a hug.

"What do we do now?" she asked.

"Let's sit back and do some planning." Mike started to turn away, and then looked back puzzled.

"Have you ever been this far down the valley before?"

"No I was always turned back long before this."

"Look down there." He pointed toward the edge of the valley where it turned in below them. That stand of trees is not natural, there planted, and I think at least one of them is a fruit tree."

Paula looked, careful not to break through the cover of the trees. "That must be the Williams homestead," she answered. "I never knew where it was. I should have guessed. They were the protectors of the valley, guarding the entrance to the cave."

"Let's scout around behind in the cover of the bush, and we may be able to stock up on at least some fruit."

Paula answered him with a hug, and they carefully made their way around the bush edge until they found themselves looking down on the barn directly behind the homestead. Careful to stay out of sight of the cave they descended the slope. Mike stopped at an apple tree and picking a ripe looking one, passed it over to Paula, before getting one for himself.

"Should we take a look inside?" Paula whispered softly.

He shrugged. "Why not, we might find something interesting."

The house was of a similar layout to the Kennard's, but had an extra set of rooms back off the lounge beside the kitchen, making it more of a "U" shape, as opposed to the "L" of the Kennard's. Mike availed himself of the toilet as they passed by, and they quietly entered the back door of the sleeping wing. The place smelt musty and dust had accumulated on the sparse furniture, but the building, like the Robinson's at the other end of the valley, was in very good condition. Mike felt a chill up his spine as he looked into the rooms. Beds were made, and personal artefacts sat on the tables. It was as if they were coming back anytime soon. They entered the main lounge. Chairs and tables, all intact, pictures on the wall, it all sat as a tribute to those who had once lived there. Like a museum piece, a snapshot in time, but this was real, not a posed set.

"Mike," Paula called quietly from the kitchen curtain, "You had better take a look at this."

As he entered the room, Paula pointed to the open pantry. Cheese and bread, butter and fried fish, lamp oil and other items greeted him. He looked sharply at Paula.

"This is all fresh," he whispered.

She nodded vigorously.

They both heard the creak of the boards on the porch together. Mike looked around frantically for somewhere to hide, but there was nowhere. He realised that if anyone entered the house they were trapped in the kitchen, and that was the one place they would be heading to. The latch lifted on the outside door. Mike looked at Paula, despair showed on her face. He knew he was faced with a sickening decision, give up, or fight. To give up would mean that they would be almost certainly kept as prisoners, and they may not ever get a second chance. To fight would probably mean someone would die, and Mike was no murderer. 'Would you want to marry a murderer' he thought. A voice sounded from outside. It was Marcus. "Give us hand with this damned sack, it's caught up."

Mike slipped quickly to the curtain and peeked out. Both were standing with their backs to the window unhooking a sack. He grabbed Paula and unceremoniously yanked her through the kitchen curtain and then in through the one beside it. They found themselves in a little alcove with two doors, one open and one closed. Mike again pushed her into the open room and in behind the door. Quickly he slid in beside her, squashing her in the corner. Footsteps sounded in the lounge and stopped. 'Had they seen the curtains moving as they came in?'

They both stood very still, desperately trying hard to control their breathing and racing hearts. The footsteps continued, then the sound of something being scraped on the table.

"Did you leave the pantry doors open last time?" came Urgut's voice.

Mike heart sank. 'Fool, fool, fool,' he admonished himself under his breath for not closing them.

"I don't think so, is anything missing?"

There was a moment's silence. "No I don't think so," came the reply.

"Must have."

"You're getting forgetful in your old age, you old codger."

Mike heard the pantry door close, and listened as the footsteps crossed the room and then the outside door latch. He let out a sign of relief, and stepped out. Paula had not moved. He looked at her. She crouched trembling against the wall, tears running down her face. She slowly sank to the floor. In a moment he was kneeling at her side. She looked into his face and collapsed into his arms sobbing quietly. It was at least ten more minutes before they ventured out of their hiding place.

"I'm sorry for being so weak," she said, embarrassed by her actions.

Mike gave her a hug. "That's alright darling, you are stronger that most women I have ever known."

They carefully moved across the lounge and looked out. Trails of dust headed up the side of the mountain towards the cave.

"Let's get some food, and get out of here."

Paula slipped into the kitchen and soon emerged with some cheese, bread and dried fish.

"I only took a little of each," she said, "It doesn't look too obvious that stuff is missing."

They slipped out the back and gathered some fruit as they walked through the orchard, then disappeared into the bush line.

A small stream ran down through a little gorge and passed the homestead before it merged with the main river, and as they crossed it on their way back to the campsite, Mike stopped for a drink.

"Do you hear that?" he asked Paula.

She listened, "It sounds like a waterfall, further up," she replied.

"Let's take a look."

"You're on to something aren't you?"

He gave her a wry smile. "Maybe, just maybe."

They followed the stream up for about another 250 yards. The noise of the waterfall was now so loud as to make normal speaking difficult, then as they pushed through a patch of Whiteywood, it stood before them. About 50 feet high and 10 feet across it poured over a sheer drop to plummet unimpeded into the pool below. The walls on either side created a bush-shrouded amphitheatre around the pool. Native orchids and moss hung from the surrounding trees and epiphytes filled the crooks in every bough. Birds flitted between the trees picking bugs out of the air, and native fish, swam in the clear water. They stood awestruck by the beauty of nature.

Something else was now however catching his eye. Paula, also dumbfounded by the beauty of the place, turned to look at him. He had a strange knowing kind of smile. "OK. What do you see that I don't?"

"Watch the mist around the sides of the waterfall."

"It's swirling. So?"

"It's more than swirling, it's breathing."

Paula stared for a moment then saw what he was talking about. The mist seemed to sometimes get drawn back behind the wall of water, other times it seemed to puff out.

"I bet there is a cave behind there and it has passages that are connected to other passages that come out into the valley. The wind travelling through them is sucking or blowing the mist around the edges of the waterfall."

Mike stripped to his underwear and waded into the water.

"Wow, that is cold," he gasped as he dipped his body in. "I'll be back in a moment."

Paula watched as he swam to the rocks on the left of the deluge, then suddenly he disappeared into the water. She waited for several minutes and was getting to the point she was going to go in to look for him, when he re-emerged and swam across to her. Grinning from ear to ear he wrapped her in a wet embrace and swung her around several times before putting her now wet body down.

She did not care. "Well?" she asked fervently, holding his hands in hers.

"I think it's our way out," he said and hugged her again.

Mike dried himself off the best he could. "Shouldn't be a problem, since I was your towel," Paula chided in mock annoyance.

He stuck his tongue out at her and got dressed, then they returned back to the campsite.

"It's getting dark, so I suggest we get comfortable, get some sleep, and get going early in the morning".

"You're a real go getter, aren't you?" she quipped.

"Aren't you?" he replied just as quickly.

She gave him a squeeze, and they watched the sun go down together.

They did not see it until it was completely dark, a gentle orange flickering glow on the side of the mountain.

"They have a fire going," Mike said, a touch of jealously creeping into his voice.

"Don't they care if see where they are?" answered Paula.

"They probably want us to see it. A beacon for us to aim for."

"What do you think they would do to us if they had caught us?" she asked.

Mike thought for a moment. "Nothing physical; I mean they want us to stay alive to populate the valley, so they are not going to hurt us; if that is still their goal. And right now I can see nothing wrong with that. However I think we would find ourselves very much more restrained, locked up even."

They had a good meal of bread, dried fish and cheese, followed by some of the fruit they had gathered on the way. Paula lay down with her head on her pack and closed her eyes contentedly.

Mike looked down at her lying there.

"I love you," he said again quietly to himself.

"I love you too," she replied opening her eyes to look at him.

Mike was shocked. He had not realised just how loud he had spoken, but strangely now he felt no awkwardness or embarrassment. He extended his arms out to her. She took his hands and stood up to face him. He took a few seconds searching her face. There was no sign of fear, uneasiness or apprehension as to what he might be about to say.

"Will you marry me?" Such simple words that he knew would change his whole life.

Again there was no telltale hesitation, just a wrinkling of her nose.

"Of course I will," she replied looking straight in the eyes. Then slipping her arms around him, she pulled him to her and kissed him. This time however, it was no peck on the cheek.

Minutes passed. Reluctantly they separated from their embrace.

"I'm sorry, I don't have a ring," Mike finally said, unthinkingly fumbling in his pocket for what he knew was not there. Then his hand touched something cold and metallic.

He drew out his pocket watch and offered it to her. "Will this do as an interim token of our engagement?" he asked.

She took it, and held it fast in her hand. "With all my heart," she replied and resumed the kiss from where it left off.

Mike lay back, propped up against a semi hollow stump. He looked around. The stars were so bright, and the night so clear. Below them he could hear a waterfall crashing its way over the rocks on its endless work of sculpturing the earth. Above them was the gentle sound of the wind in the leaves. All around them was the occasional call of night animals, and a distant hoot of an owl. Beside him Paula softly breathed, his arm around her. He felt the rhythmic rise and fall of her chest. It was perfect. He looked down at her, and gently stroked her face with his fingers. She smiled and nuzzled in against him, but did not wake. He thought about tomorrow, would they escape that day, or even the next.

He thought about his parents, boy were they in for a shock. Not only would they be getting back their son, but a daughter in law too. And what of Paula parents? 'Hell I hope they like me.'

He thought about…

CHAPTER 13

Both were awake before dawn. The birds had started their chorus, and the valley was just visible in the growing light. They sat and watched, as the sun touched the top of the far hills.

"This place is so beautiful."

"It's not too late to change our minds," Mike replied.

Paula looked at him. "You would live here?"

"I'd live anywhere, with you."

They sat silently for a while, and then she said, "All this time I wanted to escape, to go home, but for two years this has been my home. I never thought about how much I have come to love this valley, and Gran has never been unkind to me, nor have the boys. All they have wanted is to protect the valley, to keep it safe, and to keep it alive. Now I am deserting it; and them." Mike put his arm around her but said nothing. "Yet on the other hand," she continued, "I do miss my family dreadfully. They must have suffered so much not knowing what happened to me." Tears filled her eyes. "Oh Mike, I don't know what to do."

"If there was only me to care about, then I might be temped to say stay; but like you, my family must be frantic trying to find me. I don't want them to suffer, thinking I am dead either. We have to go," he replied.

"We could come back, couldn't we?" Paula asked pensively.

Mike thought for a while.

"Well we know how to get in. It's the getting out now that's the problem."

"Could we really make this our home?"

"I could as long as I have you, but it would have to be just us."

"And our children," Paula added.

"And our children," Mike repeated, totally shocked at himself and his total acceptance of the situation. "We will have to make up a story somehow to enable us to disappear. We can never tell anyone about this place, ever." he added.

"I agree. We will sort out our, "outside lives", then, we will come home here. OK?"

"OK," he said, and sealed it with a kiss.

They packed up their gear and started down the trail to the waterfall.

"We need to make a raft," Mike decided as they sat beside the pool.

"Surely we can swim? I'm not helpless you know."

"Not for you. I know you can look after yourself, and me," he added. "But we don't want all our clothes wet again, so if we raft them up to the waterfall and then quickly push them round the side, I think we can keep them reasonably dry."

"Oh I see. Sorry I was getting a bit precious there for a moment. I guess we still have a fair bit to learn about each other."

"We do, but so far everything I have learned, I like." Paula wrinkled her nose and looked coyly away.

Mike had soon constructed a raft of branches tied with a native flax, and a bed of fern. They tentatively put their packs on, and pushed it out. It floated reasonably well, enough to get across the pool. Mike looked at Paula. He took a deep breath. "Well let's go."

They stripped to their underwear and put their clothes in Paula's pack before gingerly wading into the water. The cold took her breath away and she nearly screamed as she slipped off the edge into deep water. She came spluttering and gasping for breath.

"You OK?" he asked, also panting.

"Yyyesss," she stammered. "Llleeeetttssss jussst get across."

Mike swam to the side of the waterfall and Paula followed. As they got to the edge where the water cascaded down on them, he pushed the raft quickly through and followed. At first Paula could see nothing but she took a deep breath and also pushed through the watery veil. She found herself in a strange almost surreal environment. Behind her the water made an opaque wall, but in front of her was a small cave, covered in moss and dripping with water. Mike was already pulling the raft up on a little shingle beach and Paula soon was out of the water too. "Let's move in a bit further away from the mist and get dry." She nodded and followed him into a larger cavern. The light here was very subdued and it took a few minutes until they could see enough to get out there clothes. Paula had a small face towel and they took turns drying each other off.

Mike looked at her. "Some things are worth waiting for," he consoled himself under his breath.

"What's that darling?" she asked.

"I said, you are worth waiting for."

She strode up to him and kissed him passionately. "You won't have to wait long. I promise you that," and by the tone of her voice, he knew she meant it.

They soon dressed and repacked. Paula removed two oil holders.

"We will need something to light them."

"No problem." and Mike removed a flint and a small tobacco tin.

"You smoke?" Paula asked.

"No, but these tins are just great for all sorts of things." He opened it to reveal a tightly packed wad of tinder. He took out a small amount and struck the flint. Sparks cascaded into the tinder and they soon had a small fire. Paula lit the wicks of the oil jars, and a soft orange flickering light filled the cave. Mike quickly extinguished the little bit of un-burnt tinder and returned it to the tin, then shouldering his pack he set off towards the rear of the cave in search of the exit. The cave went back for about 50 yards. Several passages branched off it in as many different directions.

"We make a rule, right here and now. Neither of us loses sight of the others lamp, and neither of us goes down a passage without the other. OK?" Paula nodded her acceptance. They both set off in different directions tracing the caves interior.

"Mike, I think I have found it." Paula called softly. He came over to where she was standing before a fissure in the rock about a yard wide. She put her lamp up towards the opening and the flame flickered in a breeze.

"OK. Let's check the others, but you are right, that one leads somewhere."

They soon regrouped at the fissure.

"It has to be the one," Mike conceded. He dragged his heel along the ground making a line in the dirt in the direction that they were going, then made his way through the passage. In places it got narrower and in other places wider. At one point they had to crawl through under an outcrop on their hands and knees. Paula was about 5 feet behind him when Mike stopped.

"Wow, wow, wow," was all he could say.

She came up beside him and looked up. The roof of the cavern some 100 ft above them almost shimmered in a green glow of millions of glow-worms. She gasped at the sight.

"Oh Mike." Then she realised that the floor was also shimmering with the same green glow. It took her a second to realise that she was seeing a reflection in a huge lake that filled the centre of the floor. Mike moved gingerly around the edge.

"Be very careful," he said, "these rocks are very slippery and that lake could be hundreds of feet deep."

Paula needed no prompting, she had had one near death experience with water in the last few days, and she didn't need another. Mike searched the wall but could see no obvious way out. He hoped that the air was not coming in from above. He had nearly got all the way round when Paula saw his lamp disappear. She froze. "Mike, Mike where are you?" she called a little panicked. Then a few feet in front of her a glow appeared with Mike attached.

"In here," he said and led her around an outcrop that turned almost completely back on its self. They followed that passage for what seemed like hours, and then as they entered yet another chamber. Mike called a stop and they sat down on a ledge.

"How long have we been going?" Paula asked. Mike reached for his watch. "You tell me," he answered. She looked at him quizzically then suddenly remembered. Reaching into the side pocket of her pack she took out a handkerchief and unravelled it. She examined the dog's head on the front before flicking it open.

"Your parents must love you very much," she said reading the inscription. "They do," he answered.

"Mine do too. I hope they get along alright with yours."

"If they are anything like you, I know they will."

"So?"

"So what?"

"So what's the time?"

"Oh yea. It's 12.15. Is that all?" she replied. "I thought it must be about five."

"Can you give it a gentle wind please?"

Paula did, and started to put it back in her pack.

"Might as well keep it handy we are going to use it a lot, even to know if it's night or day. And it tells me it's time for lunch." They sat on a small ledge and ate a small amount of fruit and nuts, before setting off again, but had moved on only a few yards when the lamps revealed a split in the passage. This time however both showed signs of air movement.

"What do we do now?" Paula asked. "Should we take one each?"

"No!" he replied emphatically. "We made a rule."

"I know we don't split up. So which one?"

"Well let's work it out. It we take the right path it could either join up again or it could lead somewhere else totally. If we take the left path it must get us closer to the cave entrance. We know that it must be on our left somewhere, because it started off on our left."

"But what if we are just walking in circles?"

"That's why I have been marking the floor every time we take a new passage, and we haven't yet come across one of our marks."

She thought for a moment. "Makes sense to me. Lead on."

They walked for two more hours, ducking and diving around rocks and obstacles before they came to a tee junction. This new passage was much bigger. Mike stopped just short of stepping into it.

"Left or right?" Paula whispered.

He listened for a while. "Well we have been turning left at other times, so let's just take a little look up that way, but be very quiet. This is large enough to be the main passage to the cave entrance, and if it is we will bump into the boys."

They headed off up the passage, but had not gone more than twenty yards when Mike put up his hand. He pointed to the floor. It was obvious that people had been walking there. Then he pointed to the wall. A lamp sat in a bracket just by his left shoulder.

"We are here in the main passage for sure. This confirms it. But we are going the wrong way, we need to go back, deeper in to find the rail tunnel," he whispered to Paula.

They quietly retraced their steps back passed the tunnel they had not long exited and headed deeper into the mountain. Mike was now starting to recognise landmarks from eight days ago when he was captured. Paula however recognised nothing. He stopped in a large cavern, and looked around. "This is where I woke up," he said, pointing to a small outcrop. "They could not have carried me far, but where from is the question?"

Several passages lead off from this chamber. Most, Mike dismissed as being too small to carry someone through. That left just two.

"We'll try this one," he said somewhat excitedly.

The passage led down quite steeply then turned sharply to the right. They followed along for twenty or thirty yards, and Mike was about to give up when he suddenly stopped.

"Listen, do you hear that?" Mike suddenly said stopping up short.

"What is it?" she asked, "It seems to be getting closer."

There was a dull roar, then it faded away.

"That my darling is our saviour."

"A train?" she asked excitedly.

Mike smiled at her and nodded.

He traced his hand along the wall of the cave then stopped.

"Brick!" he exclaimed excitedly.

He moved his hands along seeking any loose ones, and then one shifted.

Carefully he eased it towards him, and then suddenly it was in his hand. He tried another. They were all loose.

He stepped back to get a better look, but as he did his foot caught on something. He gave it a tug and it came free sluggishly. A horrible sinking feeling came over him as he looked down, realising at the same moment that it was a trip wire. Rocks and dust were already starting to cascade down on him.

"Paula. Run," he cried pushing her away from him back into the cave.

He got one last glance of her as the rocks fell like a curtain between them.

He heard her scream once, then cut off.

At the same time he threw himself at the bricks.

In slow motion he felt them start to give, then, suddenly he was falling.

Rocks crashed all around him.

Hanging half out of the wall he heard his leg, trapped by rocks, snap.

Pain seared through his body and he screamed in agony.

Dust choked his mouth and nose. He coughed, trying to get his breath.

He wanted to cry out for Paula but nothing would come out.

He tried to move into a better position, but pain again seared through his body.

Liquid was running down his face. He tried to wipe it off, but it was warm and sticky. He tasted it. It was blood.

He put his hand up to his head and realised that it was coming from a huge gash, and he thought he could feel bone.

"Paula, Paula," he screamed as loud as he could. There was no sound except for the falling of small rocks. He moved his hand behind him and felt something cold and wet. Water trickled between his fingers. Reaching down he tore off the bottom of his shirt and soaked it in the water, then put it to his lips, sucking it out. He repeated it several times until the dryness started to leave his throat. His head was starting to throb. He felt himself starting to get very sleepy.

"Paula, I love you," he cried, then, unable to fight anymore, he slipped into unconsciousness.

Drifting in and out of reality, agonizing pain, both physical and emotional, filled his lucid moments, but he happily allowed himself to drift off into the refuge of nothingness again.

It was the rumbling that brought him back, and although he felt that nothing mattered anymore, the instinct for survival pulled him partially to his senses.

He groped around with his hand and grasped a lump of rock, then as the lighted windows started to flash past he threw it with all his force at the moving carriages. The effort caused him to cry out in pain, then he slipped back into oblivion.

Again he lay there; he had no idea for how long, hours, days, he hardly cared. A deep depression had descended on him and he just hoped now to die to remove him from the hell he felt.

Lights passed by, flashes of memory, were they real or not, he did not know.

Voices in his mind, conversations from the past all pervaded him. Sometimes he would hear Paula's voice soothing him, nursing him. He called her name, but when he opened his eyes he was still alone.

CHAPTER 14

Two men sat on the jigger. They had been pumping away on the handles, propelling it along the rails for nearly a mile; now they were halted at the entrance of the tunnel. They lifted the vehicle off the tracks and surveyed the brickwork.

"I hate tunnels."

"You're joking, aren't you? I thought they would be like a second home."

"And why would you think that?"

"I mean, well you're Welsh. Son of a coal miner's daughter and all that," he replied at the same time taking a step away from his companion.

"Right. You being a Kiwi would think that. Head the shape of a football and all." They had been together as an inspection team on this section of track for nearly five years, and they often chided each other good heartedly.

"So they reckon a rock broke the window in this tunnel?"

"Yea, a passenger reckoned that it smashed through the window right in front of him. Gave him a hell of a fright it did." They put on their hard hats, and then picking up a torch each, ventured inside looking for anything amiss. They walked slowly, scanning the walls and ceiling looking for any sign of loose bricks or places from which a rock could have come loose. The tunnel was not very old so they had been surprised at the report. They also knew that if anything was coming loose then it could be the warning sign of a much bigger failure, so diligence was needed. Lives were at stake.

Mike heard voices. Were they in his head? He did not know or care.

"Kids I reckon, rocks don't fall sideways." The voice faded away.

Halfway through and they had still found no sign of any problems. Then Athol shone his torch further in, and at the furthest extent of the beam, something caught his eye.

"Looks like something up ahead. Something's come down on the side of the tunnel."

Light flashed across his face, but he just lay there. "Another train." He half opened his eyes, and they were forced shut by the sudden pain of bright light shining directly into them. He tried to lift his arm to shield them but he was too weak.

"Stone the flippin crows," he heard someone say, "There's a bloke in here."

He vaguely saw people around him. Lights and searing pain engulfed him, but mainly, thankfully, most of all, there was nothing.

It took them over an hour to carefully dig him out of the rubble. Occasionally he would call out "Paula," before slipping back into unconsciousness. Fred and Mary were called and they arrived just as he was being carried out of the tunnel on a stretcher. The rescue teams searched all they could, but the rockslide was extensive and it was considered too dangerous to dig in any further, especially considering that his parents told them that he had been on his own that morning.

It was his mother's voice that finally brought him out of the coma.

" ... And Jean McGuire, you know her, from the store in Darby, well she ..."

"Mom?" he croaked.

"What! Mikey, oh Mikey. Fred, Fred, he's awake."

Slowly he became aware of a flurry of action all about him. "Check his breathing," he heard someone say, then he was being prodded and poked. He felt a tightening pressure on his arm, then it released.

'Hospital. I'm in a hospital,' the sounds and smells began to register, but so did the pain.

He tried to put his hand out beside him. "Paula," he whispered quietly.

"PAULA," he yelled, sitting bolt upright and opening his eyes fully for the first time. "Paula where is Paula," he frantically looked about him.

To his right stood a man in a white coat, whom Mike immediately recognised as a doctor. To his left were two nurses, and at the foot of the bed were his mother and father, holding each other, looks of anguish on their faces. He felt a person on each shoulder gently laying him back down in the bed.

"Paula, did you find Paula? Is she alright?"

"We were together in the valley."

"We were captives," … "Mike."

"We had to escape," … "MIKE."

"There was a rock fall, she ..." … "MIKE."

He looked up at the doctor. "You were alone. There was nobody with you. You have been caught in a rock fall, in a railway tunnel. And you have been trapped there for nine days."

"But, but," his voice trailed away. He sank back into the bed. "But mum I know she was with me," he cried pleadingly. "Please find her. She is on the other side of the rocks. I think she is hurt or ... Paula I'm sorry, so sorry."

Mary came up beside him, and took his hand. "We'll look, but there was no one else there. You have been in a coma for nearly ten days since they pulled you out. I thought we were going to lose you."

"Ten days," Mikes heart sank, and he knew she must be dead.

"I love her mum, I love her so much."

"Oh Mikey," was all she could say.

"Let him rest now." The doctor took her by the arm. He felt a nurse rub his arm and then a slight prick. "This will help you to sleep," she said softly.

Mike closed his eyes.

"Will he be OK?" he heard his mother say.

"He has gone through a great deal and I fear he may be suffering some mental confusion. I have a friend, a colleague who is a psychiatrist, and he may be able to help. I will give him a call in the morning." Mary gave a little gasp "You don't think he will have to go into an institution do you?" Her words were starting to float away.

"I can't say. Something is not right, but whether it is temporary of permanent, I'll leave that up to him to say …"

If they said any more, Mike did not know. He was asleep.

Over the next two days people came and went. Doctors, Nurses, Fred and Mary, Stephen and Carol, but he was distant, acknowledging them, but not wanting to talk.

Then Tony came.

Mike had been dozing, but he gradually became aware that someone was with him. He slowly opened his eyes and saw a man, he guessed in his thirties, sitting beside him, watching him. They just looked at each other for several minutes. Mike tried to remember if he had seen him before, but as far as new, the man was a total stranger.

"Do I know you?" he finally said.

"No not yet," the man replied. "Doctor Tony Blomfield."

Mike lay back. "Another doctor, which bit of me are you going to prod?"

"Actually I'm a psychiatrist."

Mike stiffened. "I suppose you are here to tell me I'm nuts."

For several moments they held each others gaze.

"Do you think you're nuts?" He waited, but Mike said nothing. "Well I don't. I'm here to help you arrive at the truth. I'm not here to tell you what that is. Only you know that. But right now you are struggling with many emotions, some you have probably not experienced before, and you need to sort them out."

"So what makes you an expert about how I feel?"

"Ever heard of Shell Shock?"

"That's what soldiers get in war, isn't it. What's that got to do with me?"

"Yes, we call it shell shock, but it is nothing to do with war. War just makes it so more prevalent. It happens when the body and mind are faced with a situation that is very traumatic, and generally can do nothing about it. They are pushed beyond their limits." He stopped and waited, assessing Mike's reaction. Mike however, was doing the same to the Doctor. He continued. "Take yourself. You have just spent nine days trapped in a dark wet tunnel, severely injured, deprived of food, proper water, no company and in incredible pain. It is a miracle you survived at all. Most people would not have. And to make matters worse help kept flashing by, only feet away. By the way, I presume it was you who threw the rock at the train?"

Mike nodded.

"That was very resourceful, and it almost definitely saved your life."

"But except for the last bit, you are quite wrong."

"In what way?" Tony asked.

"I was only trapped and injured for ..." He made a calculation in his mind recounting the days, "one day I think."

"So where were you the rest of the time?"

"In the valley on the other side of the cave system."

"And this is where you met ... ah... this girl?"

"Paula," Mike stated pointedly.

"Does she ... Paula, have a last name?"

Mike lay back thinking, racking his brain. Finally he conceded. "I don't know? I mean she must have, but I can't recall her saying it."

"But you said you loved her, didn't you? Surely if you are deep in a relationship, you would know her last name?"

"I guess I didn't ask. I didn't have a lot of time." Mike looked away and stared at the bed.

"That's alright," Tony put his hand on Mikes shoulder. "We will talk again later." Mike just nodded. He was trying desperately to recall all she had ever said, but it was just not there. He realised that he only knew her as Paula.

Another two days went past. He learned that his leg was broken in three places, that he had a broken rib and a fractured skull, and he was covered in cuts and bruises. The pain had been excruciating, especially the traction for his leg, but nothing compared to the pain in his heart. At times he wished that he had not thrown that rock; that he had died in the tunnel close to Paula. He had also learned that his tramping days were probably over, and that he would most likely walk with a limp the rest of his life. His depression was getting deeper by the day.

"Hello Mike, are you feeling any better today?"

He looked up from staring blankly at the bed covers. "No," he answered Tony truthfully.

"Do you feel like talking?"

"No."

"I want to know more about this valley. Have you ever been there before?"

"No."

"But your parents tell me that you have tramped over most of the ranges for miles around, why haven't you seen it?"

"You've spoken to my parents?" he asked a little shocked and annoyed.

"Mike, I won't lie to you."

Mike looked at him sceptically.

"No I mean it. The day I lie to you, I will have betrayed the trust I am trying to build with you. I have spoken to the doctors, your family, even the guys who rescued you. If I am to help you, I need to know you."

"You think I need help?" Mike replied slightly sarcastically. Then lowering his head. "Sorry, that was uncalled for. I know you are only doing your job." Mike paused. "You think I am insane? I think others do."

"No, I don't think you are insane at all. I do know that you have suffered a very traumatic event, and that you are confusing reality, with what your mind conjured up in an effort to keep you alive. We are only just beginning to understand how complex and adaptable the mind is when under extreme stress, and I believe that because you have a strong personality, your mind has done a very good job of keeping you sane by creating a parallel world. You have created an illusion that you have retreated into to help you cope with a reality that is too painful to accept. What you need help with now, is separating the two."

"But it is too real. I can recall day by day, minute by minute all that has happened. I can tell you if you like."

"No, I don't want you to do that. That will only help to reinforce the illusion. We have to focus on the reality."

"But it is reality." Mike insisted.

"OK, tell me about the valley. How do you explain that you have tramped over all the hills in the area and have never seen it before?"

"I don't know. Anyway, I haven't tramped over EVERY mountain range in the Alps. There are hidden valleys everywhere. Get me a map and I'll find it," Mike replied a little agitated.

"Very well, that's a good idea. Let's make this a challenge for you. You tell me what you believe, and I'll help you prove it, one way or another. But the proof must be irrefutable. Any doubt and it is a no contest, OK?"

"You're on," said Mike suddenly enthusiastic.

Tony gave him a smile, and then left the ward. He went down the corridor and into a small waiting room.

"How is he?" Mary asked anxiously. Tony acknowledged Mike's father and the doctor also.

"I think he will be fine, but it will take a while. I have given him the challenge to prove all that he can. We have to be careful though, that with each failure; and of course they will all be, that we pick him up again. One at a time, slowly, slowly he will start to see that it was all an illusion. It will be painful for him, but I have high hopes of a full recovery eventually. Now you had better go and see him, and help him keep his spirits up."

Mike waited expectantly for Tony to visit him again. He so desperately wanted to find the valley, to prove to them that it was real and then they might send out a search party for Paula. Two days later Tony arrived, and true to his word, had a map of the Southern Alps of New

Zealand. The Alps are the backbone of the South Island, stretching almost the entire length of 280 miles. They are snow capped most of the year, and rugged. Beautiful in their majesty, with deep valleys and sheer rock walls. They are in some cases almost impenetrable. The Standish farm lay deep in its foothills, and it was for this reason that Mike felt confident that he would locate the valley; Kennard's Valley.

Mike folded the map to the area around the farm. It took him a while to locate it. "There, that's our farm," he pointed to a spot on the map. "See there is the railway, and here is the tunnel. I walked into it and got about half way, then got pulled off to the left and we walked for half a day in the caves ..."

"In which direction?" Tony cut in.

Mike considered. He soon realised that he did not know which direction, other than it must have been off to the left. "Somewhere between here and here under this range."

Tony looked closely at the map. "For half a day you say, in any direction from here to here, that's 180 degrees. I count about five possible valleys that meet the criteria. Which one do you think it is?"

Again he studied the map. This was not the easy solution that he had so desperately wanted.

"I'm not sure," he finally admitted, "but there will be three homesteads in it."

"The only way we can get access into those is by air."

Mike heart sank. "We're not going to do that are we," he stated sadly, then quickly added, "But what about Paula. If she exists, she will have been missing from about two years ago."

"OK, I'll do some checking." Tony gave him a thumbs-up and left.

"Oh, by the way, thanks Tony. I do appreciate it,"
Mike called after him.

Tony stuck his head back around the curtain. "That's
my job remember." He gave him a wink and disappeared.

CHAPTER 15

It was over a week before Tony returned.

"I've got good news and bad news," he said.

"I need some good news. I'm getting tired of being in this bed, and I want to go home."

"That's going to be a bit difficult with you leg hanging up there."

"It's going to be another eight weeks. But they still won't let me out will they?"

"Why not?"

"You know the answer to that. The doctors say they need a clearance from you."

"Ah, well they are right. The question is will I give it?"

They both looked at each other for several seconds sizing each other up. Mike had decided that he would trust Tony, although the term psychiatrist still bothered him. He had heard of some of the things that supposedly went on in asylums, and it scared him.

"So here is the good news," Tony said at last.

"In August 1937 a young woman named Paula did go missing in the ranges behind your farm."

"Yes, YES, YES, I knew it. I knew it had to be true. Now you have to believe me."

"Do you remember the incident?"

"Now you mention it I do. There was quite a search at the time."

"Great. I have just proved to you that she existed, and that you knew of her. Now you prove to me that you were with her, two years after she was declared dead."

Mike stared at him.

"I'm sorry Mike. The fact you knew of her means that her existence is already implanted in your mind. That means that she can be recalled as an illusion when the right triggers are pushed, such as when in Shell Shock. For you to prove that she is not part of the illusion, you need to be able to give irrefutable evidence that could not have been previously known."

Mike's head sank to his chest. "So what's the bad news?"

"I spoke to your parents and they asked a top dressing pilot if he would make a sweep over the valleys you mentioned. He did a quick look before the weather packed in, but said there was no sign of any occupation in any of them that he checked."

"He still could have missed it," Mike said dejectedly.

"Yes he could have, but it doesn't look promising."

"I think I would like to be alone now."

"I'm sorry, I wish there was an easier way. The mind can pull some cruel tricks at times, but the body will do anything to survive."

Mike lay there for hours trying to find that piece of evidence, but could not. Tony had a convincing argument, but he had not been there; had not felt her love; her touch. She was his reason to live, to carry on, he could not give up on her; not yet.

Over that next three weeks his body healed, his mind did not. He frequently had nightmares, and woke up calling Paul's name. His actions and outbursts were upsetting the other patents, so they moved him to a private room with a door.

Tony came to see him on a regular basis, but Mike seemed to be making little improvement. It was just after one of their sessions, as Tony was leaving that the doctor baled him up in the corridor, leaving Mike's door slightly ajar.

"How's he doing?"

"Not as well as I had hoped," Mike recognised Tony's voice.

"I will be ready to release him at the end of the month. His leg has mended reasonably well but he will need rehabilitation, and he will have a permanent limp. Will you be able to release him?"

"Not unless I see a marked improvement in the next week."

"And if not?"

"Then I will have to start the process of getting him committed to an institution. He is still a suicide risk. The problem is, once he is in the system; it is very hard to get out. He could be in there for years."

"What do you ..." The voices faded as they started to walk down the corridor.

Mike realised that his heart was pounding. He did not want to go into an asylum. Depressed he might be, insane he was not. If he was going to find out the truth about Paula, he could not do it if he was locked away.

Two days later Tony entered the room.

"Hello," Mike said cheerfully.

Tony eyed him carefully. "How are you? The nurses said that you were more relaxed."

"I don't seem to be having the dreams about Paula as often, and I thought about the things you said, and you are right, there is nothing I can do to prove it happened."

Tony leaned back in the chair beside him and put his hands behind his head.

"So what are you going to do when you get out?"

"I guess there is not a lot I will be able to do initially, but I can help around the house, and fix things in the workshop."

"Good its early days but I think we have reached a turning point."

It took a further week of painful rehabilitation after Mike was released from traction, before the day of his release from hospital came. His mother and father, Uncle Stephen, his wife Carol and their son Timothy, all came to help welcome him home. Tony was also invited, and watched quietly as Mike sat on the porch and gazed out over the paddocks.

"So how do you feel, now you are back at home?" he asked, after the initial turmoil had subsided.

"Great. It's so good to get out in the country again."

Tony gave him a pat on the shoulder and said goodbye, then went back in the house. He sidled up to Fred. "A quiet word maybe; out the back?"

They made their way out past the clothesline to a bench seat that Fred had made some years before.

"How is he?" Fred asked.

"I'm fairly sure that he is not suicidal, but I do have some concerns as to the nightmares. He says he is not getting them as often and that he is accepting them as an illusion brought about by the trauma; but I think he is playing down the issue. I can see real hurt and sorrow in his eyes, and I am sure he is still grieving for Paula."

"But if she is only an illusion?"

"Illusion it may be, and for us it is easy to see. But for Mike she is as real as you are to me. It was her, although imaginary, that probably kept him alive. To acknowledge her as not real, would be to kill her. Just keep an eye on him for a while. That's all."

"Thanks Tony, I will."

A week went past. Mike did a few chores around the farm as best he could on crutches, and all appear to be going fine, until one evening when they were sitting in the lounge listening to the radio.

"What's the time?" Mary asked.

124

Automatically Mike put his hand in his pocket. His fingers clutched at nothing. He pattered his other pockets, then suddenly stopped and stared straight ahead.

"I said Wha …; Mike are you OK?"

"Mike?"

"Oh … sorry, I must have lost it in the tunnel."

"Oh dear, you did love that watch so, I'm sure we can get you another one made."

Mike just nodded, and said nothing.

"Fred," Mary said about 10 the next morning, "have you seen Mike today, he hasn't been in for breakfast?"

"No, I'll check his room." Fred returned a few moments later, "No he's not there, he might be out in the yards."

Mary heard him calling Mike, but there was no response. Finally Fred came back inside. His car is still here, he might have gone down the road to the neighbours, or he might just need some time alone."

"I'm worried," Mary took Fred's hand, "Is he going to be alright? Last night he seemed so distant again."

Fred sighed. "Let's give him a couple of hours and if he is not back we will call for help, OK?"

Mary gave his hand a squeeze and nodded.

CHAPTER 16

Sleep had eluded Mike for most of the night, and when he did, he dreamed of Paula. He knew he had given his watch to Paula as an engagement token, but in the caves they had exchanged it back and forth many times, and he could not remember who had it last. Maybe it was in the tunnel, in the rubble where he lay, but maybe it was with Paula. At times he could see her broken body buried under the rocks. At other times he could see her back with Gran and the boys, destined to die alone at some time in the future. By dawn he had made up his mind. He had to find out or go mad.

Quietly he made his way out of the house to the implement shed. The sun was just on the horizon as he hobbled on his crutches, a spade slung across his back on a piece of rope, across the road to the paddock that led down to the railway. He eyed up the seven-wire fence. There was no way he was going to be able to climb it, so he dropped the spade on the other side, then laying on his back, he squeezed under the bottom wire. He pulled his crutches through after him, and retrieving the spade made his way down. Initially it was not a big problem, but soon he realised that crutches and a slippery steep grass slope were not compatible. He considered his options, and giving up was not one of them. He gave a sigh then sat down and foot-by-foot, yard-by-yard, he slid down the grass on his backside dragging the spade and crutches behind him. The task took nearly an hour, and by the time he reached the bottom fence by the railway he was exhausted. Mike rested for ten minutes, then following the same procedure that he had at the top, slid under the fence. There was a small track beside the rails, but it was very rough and progress was agonizingly slow for him, but still he pressed on towards the tunnel.

Two hours later he stood at the bridge. Once across he was only 200 yards from the entrance. It was tricky enough for an able bodied person to walk across having to step over the gaps between the sleepers, and negotiate the guide rails that ran between the main rails; also there was no hand rail to balance you if you stumbled. For Mike, on crutches, and exhausted, it was a major obstacle. Maybe it was adrenaline or courage, or sheer stupidity that drove him on, but he almost made it across, with only 10 yards to go when he heard the blast of a steam whistle. It echoed around the valley and initially he could not tell which way it had come from, then he also heard the sudden roar of the engine and he knew it had just exited the tunnel in front of him. He had only seconds to get off the bridge and he knew it. Throwing caution and pain to the wind he frantically pushed himself forward only partly using the crutches and putting a lot of weight on his shattered leg. The pain almost caused him to fall, but he forced himself to cover the distance; then with 2 yards to go, the train appeared around the bend. The fireman must have seen him and he pulled hard and long on the whistle. Mike did not wait to get off the last bit of bridge. He jumped over the side into the long grass and rolled down to the edge of the creek. He lay there spasms of pain surging through his body, his heart pounding in his chest.

It was nearly half an hour before he tentatively crawled his way up the slope to the level ground beside the track. He retrieved the crutches and the spade from where he had thrown them, and eased himself to his feet. His leg hurt like hell and he hoped he had not done any serious damage to it. Mike stood there for a few more minutes, taking deep breaths, then slower that before started off again for the tunnel entrance. He stood looking into the darkness for quite a while. A mixture of fear, exultation and trepidation filled him, but he had come too far to turn back now. He turned on his torch, and hobbled into the tunnel. He took another half hour to reach the alcove where a few weeks before he had been laying, injured and dying. The situation now seemed surreal as he approached the newly cemented brickwork.

"'How am I going to get through this" he muttered to himself. And why didn't I bring a pick?" It was only now, confronted with this obstacle that he realised just how ill conceived his plan and his preparations had been. He took the spade and jammed it into the brickwork, trying to crack the new mortar between the bricks. Finally after about ten minutes he managed to prize one out. Now it would be easier. He chipped away at another, and soon had it on the ground beside him. Then five more followed. He had just stopped for another rest when he was bathed in light.

"Put down that spade."

Mike turned, but could not see who was speaking.

"I said put down that spade mister."

CHAPTER 17

It was a quarter past five when Fred came in.

"Any sign?" asked Mary, panic starting to show in her voice

"No. I have driven up to the end of the road and down to the Jones place, no one has seen him. I think it is time we called for help." Fred was walking towards the phone when it rang.

"Standish Farm... Who?... What?... Where is he?... But, but, alright we come down in the morning, thank you."

Fred turned to Mary. "That was the police. Mike has been arrested for wilful damage and public endangerment. He appears in court tomorrow in Darfield."

Mary let out a little cry as she saw Mike being led into the dock. He hobbled across the short distance on his crutches and stood swaying slightly, facing the judge. His face was ashen and drawn, and he was obviously in a lot of pain.

The judge eyed him for a moment, and then signalled a court official. "Get the defendant a chair." The man obliged and Mike thankfully sat down, also thanking the judge in the process.

Mike looked around the room. In front of the judge sat the court stenographer. On the far side sat two men he had never seen before, and behind them he recognised one of the policemen who had arrested him the day before. On the near side sat his mother and father. He met his mother's anguished look and turned away, ashamed. He noted a few other individuals were in the room, but took no real notice.

A court official cleared his throat. "In the case of the Crown verses Michael John Standish. It is charged that on 27th June 1939, you wilfully damaged the inside of New Zealand Government Railways Tunnel No 57 North of Springfield in such a way that it could have caused endangerment to the public."

The judge looked across at the prosecution, then back at Mike, noting the empty defenders table.

"Mr Standish, do you not have council to defend you?"

Mike attempted to stand up, but the judge waved him back down. "No your honour, there is no need, I am guilty as charged."

The judge sat back in his chair and considered him. Then he turned to the prosecutor. "State your case."

The Council looked a little surprised at the request considering the guilty plea from the defendant, but stood up anyway.

"Very well your honour, I call my first witness, Constable McClune from the Springfield Police Station."

The Constable took the stand and was sworn in.

"Constable, can you tell the Court what conspired yesterday regarding the defendant Mr Standish."

"Your honour. At about 11.30am on the 27th June the crew of an East bound freight train nearly hit a man on crutches walking on railway property on the Wainui creek bridge. The man was seen to jump off the edge of the bridge. The train crew reported the incident at the next station and the Station Master phoned us in case the man was injured. We approached the bridge but could not find anyone, but as the witnesses said that he was heading towards the tunnel we thought we had better take a look. Of arriving at the tunnel entrance we heard the sound of someone working in the tunnel. We entered the tunnel and apprehended the defendant Mr Standish removing bricks from the tunnel wall and we duly arrested him."

The judge looked at Mike.

"Do you dispute any of these events Mr Standish."

"No your honour."

"Has this man any history of offending in the past?" he asked the prosecution.

"No you honour."

The judge again turned to Mike.

"I know your family, and you are pillars of the community. Would you like to explain your actions to me?" he asked.

Mike thought for a moment. 'What good would it do, no one believes me about Paula anyway.' "No your honour," he answered quietly.

"Then I will pass sentence."

"Excuse me your honour, may I approach the bench." The voice came from the back of the court.

"And who are you?"

"My name is Doctor Tony Bloomfield. I am the defendant's psychiatrist."

Mike was taken aback, he had not even known that Tony was in the court, but he was secretly pleased he was. He watched as the prosecutor, judge and Tony spoke quietly together.

"Well," asked the judge, "what's this about?"

"Your honour I am not here to make excuses for my client's behaviour. He is quite sane, but he is deeply confused. You may remember the events not long ago of the man trapped in the tunnel, the very same tunnel for nine days?"

The judge looked over at Mike. "Yes, I thought I knew the name from somewhere."

"Well he still is suffering for what amounts to shell shock, and believes that an imaginary woman was keeping him company, and that she is still buried in the cave beyond the tunnel. Obviously this is not true, but in his fragile state, he honestly believes that it is. Interestingly, it is this very illusion that probably kept him alive. I have been treating him since the accident, and he seemed to be getting over the trauma, but I have not had time to assess this last incident. Something must have triggered a relapse. I am asking that he not be incarcerated, as that would, in my professional opinion, be very detrimental to his recovery. Instead, if I may be as bold, suggest that he be temporarily removed from the area, and that he stay in Christchurch with his Uncle Stephen Standish, and his family for a few months."

The judge looked at the prosecutor. "Well under the circumstances we would not oppose that."

"I have already spoken with the family and they are in full agreement, if you are your honour." Tony added.

They all returned to their seats. "Very well, I release Mr Michael Standish into the custody of his Uncle Stephen Standish, on the condition that he does not make any attempt to enter the area around the tunnel 57, or trespass on any other New Zealand Government Railway property. Case dismissed. Mr Standish, you may stand down."

Mike sat dazed not really understanding what had just gone on. People were suddenly all around him. His mother gave him a big hug, and kissed him. His father and Stephen lifted him to his feet. "Let's get you back to the hospital and see what damage you have done to yourself," Fred said to him. They stopped as they passed Tony. "Thank you so much Mr Bloomfield," Mary said with tears in her eyes.

He looked at Mike. There was no life in his eyes.

"Mike," said Tony. There was no response.

"MIKE," he said again, this time getting a spark of comprehension.

"Mike, I will see you in Christchurch. We need to have a serious talk!"

CHAPTER 18

Mike spent three days in the hospital before Stephen collected him and took him home to Christchurch. X-rays showed that he had partly re-broken one of the bones in his leg, so they had to make the decision to re-set it or leave it as it was. As it transpired they decided to let it mend naturally, even though it would probably mean a slightly worse limp.

Mike said very little on the trip into Christchurch. Stephen owned a small block of land in Heathcote County to the East of the city. It was nothing like the wide-open spaces that Mike was used to, but at least it was in the country. The house was not palatial but it was quite large compared to the normal farm cottage. It had four bedrooms, a large lounge, a separate dining room, and unlike the farm they also had an inside toilet, which was quite a novelty, one that Mike later decided he would get organised for the estate when he got home. But for now he stayed mostly in his room. Timothy, Stephens's son was still living at home and being only 2 years younger than Mike did his best to befriend him. Mike was never unkind, but although he did go into town on the train with him, kept pretty much to himself.

"Just give him some time and some space" Stephen told him, "Just be a friend when he needs one."

It was a week before Tony knocked on Stephens's door. He and Mike sat on the back porch in the sun, each sipping on lemonade.

"So what triggered it off," Tony suddenly asked.

Mike had regained some of his previous spark but was still depressed and despondent.

"Something triggered a major relapse, something significant" he pressed.

"I realised that I didn't have my watch," Mike replied.

"And why is that significant?"

"I ..." His voice trailed off.

"What do you think you did with it?"

"I… gave it to Paula in place of an engagement ring."

"Ah, yes that is significant. Were you looking for the watch, or Paula?"

Mike thought for a moment, "Paula."

"What would you have done if you had found your watch instead?"

"I don't know?" Mike had not considered that alternative.

"If you had found it, could that have helped prove to you that this experience was an illusion. In reality, is there any other way that you could have lost your watch, other than having giving it to Paula?"

"I could have dropped it I suppose."

"Mike, this is important! The reality is that you were trapped in a dark wet tunnel. What is the opposite of that?"

"Open fields I guess."

"Right. You were all alone and scared. What is the opposite of that?"

"Companionship and comfort."

"Right again. So when you were trapped and alone, in pain, injured, what picture would your brain want to see to help you survive?"

What can I do, it is so real, so painfully real?" Tears were now welling up in his eyes.

Tony put his hand on his shoulder. He let him cry for several minutes before answering.

"You have to find for yourself the alternative explanations, like I have been showing you."

Tony reached into his bag and pulled out a sheet of paper with the tops and bottoms folded in.

He turned and showed it to Mike. On it was a picture of a woman. It was Paula.

Mike gasped. "Where, how?" He stammered.

"This is the actual poster that was put up all around the district when she went missing. You must have seen it many times." Tony opened up the top and bottom flaps. Above the face were the words;

MISSING
HAVE YOU SEEN THIS WOMAN

At the bottom it also said.

"If you see Paula Henderson, call your local Police Station".

Mike took the poster from him. "Yes, I do remember seeing this around."

"So now you know where the face and the name came from. Now you need to examine other details from your experience and find those alternatives also."

"But what if I find out that something has no explanation?"

"Everything in your experience will have an explanation; you just need to find it. For your experience to be real, you will need irrefutable proof. Something that you could only know; or have physically got, by actually being there. I would be very surprised if you found that. In fact I am sure you won't."

Mike sat back and considered what Tony had said.

"You; your brain needed to have a protection to survive. In the tunnel it created an illusion to do just that. The problem is that the illusion then became real to you.

136

Now you need, not to forget the illusion, but to create a new protection, this time based on the knowledge that it was an illusion. You will probably never forget the experience, so let it be a happy memory, not a nightmare."

Over the next month Mike's condition improved dramatically. He thought often and hard about what Tony had said. He could fully understand how his mind could have been fooled into believing in an illusion. The pain of loss and love were still as real as if he had actually known her, but he was finding that the irrational desperate urges to locate Paula and the valley, were being replaced by a more rational inquisitive side of him, that wanted to know where all the impressions that had invaded his mind had come from.

Mike reviewed the experience. He had already determined that Paula actually existed, and from where the details of her, that had been implanted into his memory, had come from. He decided to concentrate on three areas.

Firstly, were there any caves? Secondly did a valley really exist? And thirdly, where did the memory of the Kennards, Richardsons and Williams come from?

He also found that he was quite comfortable living with Stephen and Carol. Initially he had been annoyed that the decision had been made to place him there without consulting him, but he realised that it had probably kept him out of jail, and now he was in the right place to do his research. Christchurch was New Zealand's third largest city and held all the records for most of the South Island, so getting access to information was going to be much easier. Mike decided to start with finding the valley first.

By now Mike and Timothy were becoming good friends, and Timothy was keen to help Mike as best he could, so on a cold late August morning, they trudged the mile to the railway station and headed into Christchurch, and the land office. They looked first at the titles of the owners surrounding the tunnel area. The Standish farm and those on the Alps side were all accounted for and bordered on the railway. Beyond that was wilderness and all ownership was the government's. Next they examined all the survey maps of the area, but although these showed the valleys he had already identified, none stood out as being the one he had seen in his illusion. They returned home that afternoon a little discouraged being unable to make any tangible progress.

The next day Mike phoned Tony about it.

"I understand your reasoning, but what happens if I cannot find proof, or an explanation?" he asked.

"We are talking about a valley, right?, a very special valley in fact."

"Yes."

"Have you ever been in a valley like it anywhere? Maybe some place that really impressed you greatly?"

Mike thought for a minute. "There is a valley in Southland that I really love going to."

"Is it in any way like the valley in your experience?"

"Yes, I guess it is, but it is uninhabited."

"Remember Mike, an illusion is like a dream but more intense, more precise, but it is still an experience made up of retained information in your brain. It is not always exact. The fact that you like this real valley is likely to be the picture, although not exact, that your brain has built the illusion on. It then added people and buildings, probably all images from past experiences, and assembled them into a believable story for you. A world that you were able to retreat into, away from the pain and loneliness you were experiencing. Does that make sense?"

"Unfortunately it does, but thanks anyway."

"Keep searching Mike and you will find the truth and the peace you are seeking.

Now however there was another concern affecting Mike, but not only him, the whole nation. There was mounting concern about the events unfolding in Europe. Hitler had invaded Czechoslovakia causing it to split in two, and there were rumours of a pending war. He knew that if there was a major conflict, New Zealand would likely be involved as it had in the First World War. He worried how this would affect his family.

The next day was the 3rd September. It was late in the evening, when the radio brought the news no one wanted to hear. In a broadcast from Neville Chamberlain, the Prime Minister of Great Britain, he said:

This morning the British Ambassador in Berlin handed the German Government a final note stating that unless we heard from them by eleven o'clock that they were prepared at once to withdraw their troops from Poland, a state of war would exist between us. I have to tell you that no such understanding has been received and that consequently this country is at war with Germany.

"Well that's that," was all Stephen said as he turned and walked out of the room.

CHAPTER 19

Mike was determined not to let this affect his research, and decided he would try and get information on the three families that supposedly inhabited the valley. The title searches for the names had brought up nothing. In fact it seemed that the three families really did not exist except in his mind, but some little distant bell was occasionally ringing. There was a Williams family that had settled around Greymouth in the late 1880's, but that did not match the criteria, and the land was still in the family name. As far as the Richardsons and the Kennards were concerned, no records of any settlement in the South Island, under those names were recorded.

Mike was now making weekend trips back to the farm to help out his father Fred, but Tony had suggested that he not live there for at least another year, or until he was completely convinced that his experience had been an illusion. Mike knew that he needed to get more answers to his questions before he would feel comfortable being that close to the place where he still felt that he had deserted Paula. Fred had hired extra help to work on the farm in Mike absence. They were always fully supportive of him, and his quest, talking regularly together about how he was progressing in his research.

Mike no longer talked to anyone about his experience, other than to acknowledge that is was an illusion, but he still could not disguise the loss and love he felt for Paula.

It was one Saturday afternoon that Mary gave him his first real lead. "If these people did exist, no matter where they settled, they would have come over on a ship. Have you checked the immigration or shipping resisters?" she asked.

"No, I hadn't thought of that. Thanks, I will when I get back to Christchurch."

So it was that later that week, he and Timothy went to the immigration office to look at the registers.

"No luck today," Timothy sighed, stretching his back. "Are we sure of the dates?"

"No not really."

"Could they be earlier?"

"What names were you looking for?" a voice sounded from behind a large kauri counter. The clerk poked his head up and looked across to where they sat at a large document table.

"Kennard, Richardson or Williams," Mike replied.

The clerk tapped his fingers on the bench top. "That name Richardson seems familiar. I came across it a few days ago in a much earlier register, but there was something not right about it. I just can't remember I'm sorry. It may be totally the wrong people."

"That's OK," replied Mike, "we'll get going now, thanks for your help."

"Leave me your contact details, and if I find anything I'll let you know."

Timothy gave the man his phone number and address and they left.

"Do you think he will find anything?" Timothy asked as they sat down in the carriage.

"Probably not, he has better things to do."

The guard blew his whistle; there was a clang and a slight lurch, and the train pulled out of the station.

For the next few months Mike spent a fair amount of time at his home with his parents. The nightmares had all but ceased and his desire to go to the tunnel had also waned. Fred and Mary still kept a close eye on him and Tony visited him every month to monitor his progress.

That Christmas he did find very hard. No matter what anyone said or did, Paula was never far from his thoughts, and he still grieved for her as if she had been real in his life.

Timothy got a job with a fencing contractor, and although the work was sometimes spasmodic, it helped with the income for the family. Mike was still on a sickness benefit from which he paid board to Stephen, and also helped out on jobs he was doing, just to pass him tools or other items.

It was in late August 1940 when, after supper Stephen came into the living room, he had a grim look on his face.

"What's wrong?" Carol asked looking up from the darning she was doing.

He had half a dozen letters in his hand. They watched as he shuffled through them, then he gave one to Timothy and two to Mike.

"What? What's wrong?" Carol asked again, this time to all of them. Mike and Timothy both looked at each other and then at Stephen.

Timothy was the first to open his; he looked up at his mother. "I've been called up," he said.

Mike opened his. "I have been also. What good am I with this gammy leg? But I will call Tony, he will know what to do."

"What's in the other letter?" asked Timothy.

Mike opened it and quickly read the brief note, surprise growing on his face. He looked across at Timothy. "Its from that clerk at the immigration office, I never thought I would hear from him again. He says he has found all three families, but I had better go in and see him."

Tony called in the following day. He collected Mike's call up papers and took them with him. His final statement to Mike on leaving was quite emphatic. "You will not be going to war!"

The requirement for both was to present themselves at the recruitment office at Burnham Army base two weeks later, and as Mike had heard nothing to the contrary, both he and Timothy arrived at the specified date and time. Timothy stood before the sergeant seated behind a large wooden desk. "Name and address," he stated gruffly.

"Timothy Walter Standish, Stockyard Lane, Heathcote."

The sergeant looked through his papers and then selected one. He read the contents quickly. "Step over with them," he indicated to his right to where a group of about twenty stood nervously.

Mike stepped forward.

"Name and address."

Michael John Standish," Mike hesitated, which address should he use.

"Well surely you know where you live?"

The letter came to Stephens's address he reasoned. "Stockyard Lane, Heathcote," he replied.

The sergeant looked through his file of papers. He looked again at Mike then looked through a pile of letters in a tray to his left. He pulled one out and opened it.

"Walk over to that wall and back," he demanded.

Mike complied, his limp obvious.

The sergeant put the paper back in the envelope and handed it to Mike.

"You are permanently exempt from all service. Get out of here," he said with some disdain in his voice. "Next."

Mike went over to Timothy and hugged him.

"Be careful, we need you back," he said, and with a tear in his eye returned to Stephens.

The next day to their surprise and joy, Timothy returned home fully kitted out for war.

"I just have to wait and they will tell me when I start training, sometime in the next two weeks," said Timothy, then added, "What was in that letter? That sergeant was quite miffed at it."

"It was from the Army Office and it just said that they had received letters from both the hospital and the Mental Health service saying I was permanently unfit for any duties."

"And the outcome of the other letter?"

Mike looked at him and cocked his head on one side. "Oh that letter," suddenly comprehending. "I have not had time to go in and see him."

"Then let's go tomorrow."

As soon as they entered the office, the clerk beckoned them over. "I knew there was something unusual, here look at this." He showed them the arrival date and the ship they were on.

Williams Godfrey and his wife Myrtle
Richardson Charles and his wife Elspeth
Kennard Reginald and his wife Martha

"And these are there immigration documents."

They looked down the columns. Mike suddenly felt a cold chill down his spine. He and Timothy stared at each other and then back at the document.

For each entry, under the heading "Residing at" the notation said: DECEASED.

CHAPTER 20

"What does that mean?" Mike asked.

"Well, they came over on a settlement scheme, and would have been allocated a piece of land. I would say that before any of them took possession of it they were killed."

"All three families?"

"That's why I thought it funny at the time, but there you have it."

"What if they had moved away to another area, a city maybe, and not moved onto the allocated block?" asked Timothy.

"It would still be noted here," replied the clerk.

The two men thanked him and slowly made their way back to the station. They boarded the train and sat in silence, rocking to the gentle sway of the train.

"I guess that really closes that avenue. The Kennard's I knew would have to be their ancestors, and dead people don't have children. That means the ones I met, or thought I met, must have been an illusion, and if that is so, then everything else has to be also. I guess Tony was right." Mike said at last.

"I'm sorry," was all Timothy could say.

"That's all right, at least I have proved it to myself, and that is what Tony said I needed to do. He was right I guess, but I still grieve for Paula."

He paused for a while. "I do sometimes wonder where I got those names from though."

One week later Timothy left for 3 months training at Burnham. Then after an all too short stay at home he was deployed on the 5th January 1940, with the 2nd Infantry

Division of the New Zealand Expeditionary Force to the Middle East. This was a tough time for both the families. An occasional letter came and told of mud, and turmoil, and death.

Then on 15 May 1941 another letter came, this time from the Army. Stephens's hands were trembling as he opened it. Carol sat and cried, guessing its contents.

Mike watched his face, tears in his own eyes, and so was surprised to see Stephen smile.

"Timothy has been wounded, he is in a hospital in England, and he is expected to be sent home in the next two months."

The whole family was there to meet the train as it pulled into Christchurch station.

Mike's parents had also come over to welcome him home. They knew that he had been discharged from the army because of his wounds, but did not have any details, other that he was not on a stretcher. Even so they were still shocked when they saw him. At seeing Carol he ran to meet her and dropping his bag put his arm around her. The others stood back a little; his left arm was missing from just below the elbow.

After that, Mike and Timothy became even closer, almost inseparable as friends. Now it was Fred and Mary's turn to repay some of the kindness that Stephen and Carol had shown to Mike.

By now Tony had given Mike a clean bill of mental health and Timothy was able to stay with him on the farm to recuperate. Whereas Mike was now fit to do limited work, it was Timothy who would be on a permanent war pension.

It was a Saturday afternoon, and the two were sitting on the porch looking out over the fields at the mountains.

"I now understand how you felt in the tunnel," Timothy suddenly said.

Neither looked at the other.

"I lay in the bottom of a trench, at night, looking at the flesh and bone that had once been my arm. It didn't even hurt to start with. I didn't even think it was mine. It was like looking at some other poor soldiers wound. I just watched as the blood flowed out onto the ground, and did nothing. It was another soldier, I don't even know who, that wrapped a tourniquet around my arm and called the medics. I think I would have just watched my life flow away."

"How did it happen?"

"There were two of us in the lookout post. I was watching the right sector and Nigel the left. Everything had gone quiet. We waited for a minute then sneaked a look over the top, but we could see nothing. Then there was a whole barrage of fire all around us. Nigel was looking out to his left, and in all the noise did not notice the machine gun strafing our position. I saw the bullets hitting the ground and ducked down, then I realised that Nigel had not; so I put my hand up and pushed his head away. That's when the bullet hit my arm." Now Mike looked at his cousin. "It was his head or my arm." Timothy said quietly.

Their eyes meet and he just nodded. Mike got up and went inside and came out with two beers. He opened one and passed it to Timothy, then opened his own.

"Did you ever work out where you got those names from?"

Mike frowned. "Names?"

"Yes, you know; the Kennard's."

"No I didn't. I just have to accept that as a dead end."

"Wasn't there a reference to another family in Greymouth? I thought at the time that we could follow it up."

Mike sat back and took another sip on the bottle.

"Williams," he said

"Hey we could drive over and see them, I am getting bored not having any adventures."

"Well I guess it wouldn't hurt."

"How are we going to do this?" Timothy asked. "We only get a couple of gallons of petrol a month per vehicle with rationing and all."

Mike smiled. "This is a farm, in the middle of nowhere. Don't you think we would have a drum or two of petrol on hand? And if you were to put on your army uniform..."

Mike arranged the following week off, and on the Monday they put some gear in his truck, and headed towards Greymouth.

From Springfield the road led west through the foothills and climbed up to Lake Lyndon. Here they stopped and poured a coffee from one of the several thermos flasks that they had brought with them. The "West Coast Rd" had arguably been the most dangerous road in New Zealand. Finally completed in 1865, it wound its way through the Southern Alps, but was barely useable at the best of times. However in the late 1930's it was decided to properly maintain the road although it was still classed as dangerous. Before them was Porters Pass. The pass rose 3,100 feet above sea level, and although the highest point, was by no means the worst part of the trip.

Several road construction trucks past them by. Due to the war, a concerted effort was being made to upgrade the road in case the Japanese invaded from the west, and the military needed better access. This was good for the boys in one way. If they broke down or got stuck, they were sure of help, but it also meant long delays stuck behind graders and bulldozers.

Topping the pass they descended slightly to Castle Hill. Here they availed themselves of some refreshment at the local hotel, before again winding their way down the valley past Lake Pearson and on to Cass. This was the first point since Springfield that the railway met up again with the road, and was as such, an important town. However, once they left there, the road would become much more difficult. A new bridge over the Waimakariri River had taken a lot of the danger and strain on both vehicle and human on this notorious portion of the trip through Bealey flat, and they again did not miss the opportunity to show their appreciation by exchanging some money for liquid refreshment at the Bealey Hotel.

They would have liked to spend more time in this beautiful rugged valley surrounded by high snow capped peaks and sheer rock bluffs, but they wanted to get to Otira before nightfall, and the worst of the road was yet to come. From this point at the end of the Bealey Flat, the road started to climb again steeply until it topped the main divide at Arthurs Pass. They did not stop here, but started the most dangerous part of the road, the descent to the Otira River via the infamous Zigzag. This bit of the road was cut out of nothing more than a huge shingle slide, and dropped 540 feet down from Peg Leg Creek to Candy's Bridge in a series of hair-pin bends on grades as high as 18%. Any failure of brakes on the way down, or a stall on the way up, could send you straight down into the Otira River below.

It was late in the day when they pulled into Otira Township, and booked into the hotel.

Otira was now a major town supporting the railway. This was the western end of the Otira rail tunnel and a place where electric power was produced, and the locomotives serviced, for the short electrified section up to Arthur's Pass. This section of the Midland Line was so steep, a 1 in 33 grade, that it was impractical for steam locomotives to negotiate, so electric banker locomotives were coupled on, to pull the trains through the 5.3 mile long tunnel.

Mike and Timothy ate a hearty meal, despite this being wartime and many things being rationed. But this was also a very remote country outpost, self-sufficient and resourceful. Having come from the farm, Mike had had the forethought to take some beef with him, and they exchanged a whole rump and hind leg for their nights stay. At the same time they had made instant friends with the hotel owner, and were assured of a room on the return journey. They settled in for the night amid the clanking of shunting railway wagons.

After a good nights sleep, and a breakfast of wild bacon and farm eggs, they headed off towards Greymouth. The road now was almost level and the going much easier. They stopped at the settlement of Jacksons for a coffee before carrying on to Kumara Junction. Here the Otira Highway met the Kumara Junction Highway to Hokitika, and the Taramakau Highway to Greymouth. They turned right and arrived in Greymouth just before nightfall. This town was, as the name suggested, at the mouth of the Grey River. Greymouth was the predominant town on the West Coast, and a major port servicing the gold, coal and timber industries that prospered throughout the region.

The next day they headed for the Post Office to make enquiries as to the location of the Williams homestead. After sorting through a number of false leads, they located it on the road to Taylorville, and set off across Cobden Bridge over the Grey River heading north. At Coal Creek they turned right and followed the Grey inland. It took them nearly an hour before they came to a sign: Williams Estate. Mike stopped at the end of the drive. He could not see the house from the road but he assumed that it lay sheltered behind a stand of Macrocarpa half a mile up the hill. The farm was much flatter than theirs. Though still rolling, it stretched further back into the hills, up to the bush edge. He and Timothy looked at each other, then with a shrug drove over the cattle stop and up the drive. They were met by five dogs, which announced their presence in no uncertain terms. Both knew better that to get out around unfamiliar canines, so sat in the truck. They did not have to wait long.

The door opened to reveal the most beautiful woman that Timothy had ever seen.

Tall and slim with long flowing auburn hair and green eyes that shone like emeralds.

"Close your mouth, you're dribbling," Mike chucked as he got out and approached her.

"Excuse me; I'm looking for the Williams family that moved to Greymouth from England around 1830."

"I don't look that old do I?" she said with a wicked little grin.

"Most definitely not," answered Timothy as he approached having finally stopped staring and had stumbled out of the truck.

"Thank you. Just a moment please," she went back inside. A few moments later a man came up the hallway.

"Can I help you gentlemen?"

This was a big man. He filled the doorway both by height and width. Mike swallowed.

"We are looking for the Williams family that moved to Greymouth from England around 1830. Well actually not them, but a Williams family that may have come out 2 years before," he stammered a bit awkwardly.

The man looked them up and down.

"You local? I haven't seen you around these parts."

"No. Oh sorry I'm Mike Standish and this is my Cousin Timothy. We live on the other side of the divide," he replied extending his hand. Mike was no weakling, yet as they shook hands he was sure that this man could have crushed his in a second if he had wanted to.

"Stanley," he said by way of introduction. "Come a long way then. Better come on in." He led them down the hall to the lounge. It was much bigger that Mike's place. Three couches formed a "U" shape around one side, and looked out through a large set of glass doors over the valley beyond. They sat down.

"Lucy," the man called, and a middle-aged woman came and stood in the door.

"Can we have a cuppa please?"

"Tea?" she asked.

The boys nodded in unison.

As she left, she was replaced in the doorway by the girl.

"You have met my daughter Susan." She came across the room and sitting down opposite Timothy looked him up and down.

"What happened to your arm?" she asked bluntly.

"I had it blown off in Egypt last year."

"Oh sorry," she said suddenly sounding a little embarrassed.

"It's no big thing. I'm glad I'm right handed though."

"Were you with him?" Susan asked Mike. For the first time since the war began, he felt suddenly ashamed that he had not gone to fight also.

"No I smashed my leg badly a few years ago, and I am permanently disabled."

"Oh," she said. Mike noticed that she had not taken her eyes off Timothy, nor he hers.

"Here we are." Lucy put a tray on the table and started pouring out the tea.

"So you are interested in Godfrey and Myrtle. May I ask why?"

Mike's jaw dropped. "You know them then."

"Godfrey is… was my father's brother."

Mike slumped back into his seat. "Do you know what happened to them?"

"And can I ask you again, why?"

"Actually it's not just them exactly. It's three families I am trying to find information on. They went missing somewhere near our farm, maybe even on it. They were the Williams, the Richardsons and …"

"The Kennards," Stanley finished the sentence for him.

Silence filled the room. Mike and Timothy stared at each other in disbelief.

Then Stanley spoke again. "Well there is not that much to tell. All three families were friends in England and applied to come out here together. They were allocated land on your side of the Alps. As far as we know they went in to claim their blocks and disappeared."

"Disappeared?" Mike asked leaning forward in his seat.

"Well they just vanished. Never seen again, and eventually pronounced dead."

"You mean the bodies were never actually found?"

"No not a sign. They just disappeared."

Mike looked at Timothy. Timothy however was now having his own wordless conversation with Susan.

Mike sat back again. What did it mean he thought? Did he have the answer to the mystery? He decided to say nothing more until he could check things out further when they got back.

He started talking about farming and soon was having a great conversation with Stanley about, cows and sheep and pasture types. Occasionally he would look at Timothy, but he was now fully engaged in real conversation with Susan and her mother. He smiled. This was a whole different side of his cousin that he knew nothing about. 'Suave little cuss. He can certainly make an impression with the ladies,' he thought to himself.

"You can't leave without a meal," Stanley insisted about 4 pm.

"Come on, I'll show you around the farm while the ladies do their thing."

It was well after nine when they said their goodbyes. Stanley had suggested that they stay the night, but as Mike pointed out, to Timothy's dismay, they had already paid for their room in Greymouth.

Mike checked that the blackout covers were fitted to the headlights securely, and as he got in noticed Susan slip a piece of paper into Timothy's hand. They had a slow trip back. The slits may have stopped aircraft from seeing them, but it also stopped them seeing the road. Back in the hotel with the curtains drawn, Timothy opened the piece of paper.

"It's her phone number," he answered the unasked question, grinning stupidly.

Mike had to turn away to stop from laughing. "She's got her hooks into you."

"I hope so," Timothy replied.

The next day they retraced their steps back to the farm. Timothy now had a new subject to talk about. Mike however also had new things to consider. The dead end that had once convinced him so surely that it was all an illusion, was suddenly no longer a no-exit road. It still didn't explain however how he might have known any of them before his accident.

CHAPTER 21

A few weeks later Mike and Timothy drove back to Christchurch.

"He is going to cost you a fortune in phone charges," Mike told Stephen. "Restrict him to twice a week, dad did."

Mike however did not drive straight back to the farm. He decided to do some more investigation. This time he went to the newspaper office and looked back over old reports, about the time the families who went missing.

It took him some time, but when he found it. The headline was quite obvious, yet strangely familiar.

IMMIGRANT FAMILIES GO MISSING

Three families on the Assisted Immigration Scheme have gone missing while claiming their blocks north of Springfield. Search parties scoured the area for ten days but no sign of them has been found. The names of the missing are ...

Mike sat back and reasoned with himself. The names were public knowledge. It was possible that he may have even read them somewhere, though he had no idea where. Again this was not the "Irrefutable Proof" he would need to convince anyone, including now himself, that his illusion was not just that; an illusion.

Back at the farm he told Fred and Mary about the trip and his findings.

"Hang on a minute." Fred got up and went out, returning a few minutes later with an old brown leather suitcase.

"That's granddad's isn't it?" Mike asked.

"Yea, it all his papers and the farms history. I had forgotten all about this." He rummaged through the case and extracted an old newspaper. Looking at it he handed it to Mike.

The headline hit him.

IMMIGRANT FAMILIES GO MISSING

"It's the same paper," he exclaimed.

"But look at this." Fred moved round to sit beside Mike, and then spread out an old document on the table.

Mike could see it was a survey map of the area.

"This is the original land allocation map. See this is us; Standish." Fred pointed to their farm. "But look at the other allocations further down this road."

Mike finger slowly traced down the properties. He turned his gaze in astonishment at his Father.

Their neighbours should have been Richardson, Williams and Kennard.

Mike lay in bed contemplating the facts. He now knew how he had probably got those names into his head. He remembered his grandfather having that case, and he remembered looking through it as any inquisitive young kid would have done. Although he could not recollect any of the things he had seen then, he guessed it was where the names had come from.

Now all he needed to do was solve the question of the caves. He knew they existed, but knew very little about them. By the time he was old enough to explore, the railway between Otira and Springfield was well under way.

There were other caves in the region, but the only one that interested him was the one they had cut into when constructing the tunnel. There was also a story that a rail worker had ventured in and had found a hidden valley, but it was only a rumour. Mike wanted to investigate that further.

Several months had gone by and Timothy was working most weeks on the farm to help out. Fred had lost a lot of his workforce to the war effort and had made good use of the two invalids.

Timothy also seemed to be making a few extra trips across the Alps, often by himself, so it was no surprise when he announced he and Susan were going steady.

Mike had made some preliminary investigations, and had struck up a rapport with a gentleman at the Railways Works Department in Addington, with the nickname 'Clanky'.

One grey day in September, when there was little to do on the farm, he jumped into the Ford and headed into Christchurch.

He met up with Clanky after work at the local Hotel. They chatted a while about the Railway through to Greymouth and arranged to meet again in his office the next day. Clanky recalled that he might have some of the original survey drawings of the area.

"So how did you get the name Clanky?" Mike asked as he sat opposite him in the railway cafeteria. They had been looking over some plans but had found nothing of interest, so they had retreated for a brew.

"Well when I was working on the line, before I got shoved in here," he gestured wildly around with his hand, "I always used to have a metal cup clipped on my belt. Never know when you might come across someone brewing up you know, well it used to bang around a bit. They reckoned that could hear me clanking half a mile away." The old man laughed.

"I might have a copy of the geology report though," Clanky finally said as they made their way back to the office. He rummaged through an old filing cabinet. "Here it is."

Mike skimmed through the document. "Here are the caves."

"It says that they knew about them, that they found that they could tunnel through to half way, then it turned off so they would carry on straight, no mention of a river or any other outlet; so no surprises."

"There must have been an outlet somewhere but it probably collapsed years ago, and there was no other entrance that we knew of."

"Do you know of anyone who explored that caves?" Mike asked cautiously.

"Oh you know of the rumour Eh? Well it is a bit more that just a rumour. One of the gangers decided to do some caving. Got lost for a whole day."

"Did he say he found anything?"

He reckoned that he found another entrance that led out into the bush, but he was more scared of being lost in the bush than in the cave, so he came back out the way he went in."

"He didn't mention a large valley?"

"Na, said there was a steep ravine, but the bush was so dense he didn't know where he was."

"And no one has ever found it?"

"Not to my knowledge."

Mike thanked him and headed home. Well the cave existed, but the worker had obviously not found the valley, but had he found the waterfall entrance? Mike could not be sure. Surely he would have mentioned such a feature Mike pondered. 'Was there another entrance?' he remembered another tunnel that had a draft blowing through it. He had walked through most of the bush in the area and he had never found a cave. The tunnel was full of drafts so it all fitted into the illusion.

Tony called around on his usual monthly visit, and Mike was able to say for the first time that he was now completely convinced that the experience had been an illusion that his mind had created. He had followed all the avenues like Tony had suggested, and for every one there was a possible explanation.

"So how come I have not got over the love and the grief?" Mike asked him.

"You don't."

"But it was an illusion."

"Ah yes; the event and the experience itself was an illusion. The emotion however was real. You really did fall in love with Paula, and you are suffering real grief at her loss."

Mike looked at him a little shocked. "I thought that once I had come to terms with the fact that the whole event was not real, the pain inside would go. How do I deal with this?"

"Like anybody else that has experienced the real loss of a loved one. Do not be afraid to celebrate her birthday; the day you met; the day you got engaged. Have a memorial the day she died. Everybody will handle their grief in their own way, and I think you are ready to do that now. You see, it was never my job, or intention, to take away from you the love you felt. It was real love. What I had to help you see was that fact that you did not physically meet her, or travel to a hidden valley, or have any responsibility for her death. That was the illusion."

"I have been scared to do any of that because I thought it would show I still believed the events were real."

Tony sat back in his chair and put his hands behind his head.

"Mike I don't think I need to call again, though I am here if you need me. Paula was a real person, and your feelings for her were real also, they were just out of step with time. Enjoy your memories of her; just remember the feelings are real, the places are not."

He stood up

"Goodbye Mike, I'm sure you will be just fine."

Suddenly Mike felt a whole lot better.

CHAPTER 22

1945 was a very good year in many ways for the Standish household. Between Fred, Mary, Mike, and two live-in land girls; along with occasional help from Timothy, they were doing better that most. The war had ended two years earlier, the economy was starting to move forward, and now Timothy had announced his engagement to Susan, with plans to marry the following year. That year Mike also got a special surprise. It was at Fred's 60th birthday that he announced that he was stepping aside and handing the family farm over to Mike. He and Mary had bought a little crib on the coast just south of Westport and they were going to semi retire and go fishing. Mike in turn offered to give Timothy and Susan a place to stay once they were married and Timothy a full time job helping him run the farm.

So it was that on the 18th June 1945, Miss Susan Williams became Mrs Susan Standish. Over 200 people descended on the Standish Estate from all over the world, some staying for several days in tents brought in for the event. The army also helped out on Timothy's behalf, providing kitchens, cooks and marquees. It appeared that Timothy had made a few friends that day in Egypt when he got shot, and was considered a bit of a hero especially as it was a Generals son that he had pushed out of the way, as a machine gun had strafed the trench, probably saving his life.

The whole back lawn was converted into a wedding venue. Immediately outside the back door, a platform ten foot by ten foot had been built for the wedding party and the Minister to stand on. Four white pillars, one at each corner, were decorated with garlands of flowers. The floor was green carpet, and a soft veil of white material that hung above, rippled in the breeze. A three-foot wide strip of the same carpet also covered three steps that led up to the platform, and then carried on through rows of chairs that fanned out on either side. Behind that again the farm spread out up to the bush line. To the right was the marquee, and to the left the majestic mountains of the Southern Alps.

Mike was of course Timothy's best man and he stood proudly beside his younger cousin as he reached in his pocket for the ring. He pulled it out and looked at it, and just for a moment hesitated.

Paula's face flashed before him, a lump formed in his throat, then he passed it to Timothy.

He looked at the happy pair. He had had some doubts initially about Susan. She was only eighteen when they had met, and far too beautiful to be a farmer's daughter, he thought. A mummy's girl, all frills and laces and empty headed. Now as he looked at her, she had proved him so wrong. Capable of fixing a tractor or straining a seven-wire fence; riding a horse and mustering cattle; she was a true farm girl. Now at twenty-two, she still seemed so young and naive. Mike tried to hide a sad smile. Paula would have been even younger had they been married. Both of them would have been; yet he knew they would have been mature beyond their years, with a love forged in adversity.

Timothy kissed his bride, the music played and they descended the platform. Mike cast his eyes over the throng. One set met his straight on. Mike approached.

"Are you OK?" The gaze held his. Mike knew that his hesitation had not gone unnoticed by at least one person.

Mike nodded. "Yes, thanks to you I think."

Tony smiled as they shook hands.

162

The next day Timothy and Susan left on a month long honeymoon to Wellington, first taking the train to Christchurch, then the ferry from Lyttelton on the eleven-hour trip to the Capital. They planned their return the same way, arriving on July fourteen.

Mike knew things were going wrong two days before. The mountains can be a beautiful environment to live in, but they are also unforgiving. Strong nor' westerly winds can snap mature trees like matchsticks, and snow can catch out the unwary, trapping them in an icy tomb.

It had been snowing for most of those two days, but the barometer was not holding steady. On the afternoon of the thirteenth it fell dramatically. Mike and Fred spent much of that evening out in the paddocks closest to the homestead, making sure that the stock had shelter. Those in the more distant hills would have to fend for themselves. When his grandfather had started clearing the farm, he had made it a policy that he would, in every paddock, leave a stand or two of mature trees to provide a refuge from wind sun and snow. Some had laughed at his approach, as total clear felling, leaving nothing more that clean empty fields, was the normal method. Some did not even leave shelter belts along the fence lines, a folly that proved to be the undoing of some in the winter of 1918. Hard on the heels of the First World War, a severe snowstorm struck the region. Many lost most, if not, all their stock.

That was the year before Mike was born, but his father had told him about it many times, and what signs to look for. He saw those signs now. The wind had dropped to nothing, and an uncanny silence pervaded the hills. It was as if he had stuffed cotton wool into his ears. All sounds, even his own, were muffled. The whole world appeared to be like an old vinyl record running at half speed, every movement was in a kind of slow motion. It was like nothing he had experienced before. By the time he got back to the homestead it was just on dark. He collected the two land girls from their quarters, and brought them into the house to sleep. He also put the house cow in the barn and checked that all the other domestic animals had shelter, then, as he walked back inside, he glanced at the outside thermometer. It had dropped another degree.

Mike did not sleep much that night. The silence was defending, broken only by the occasional woomph of snow falling off the roof.

He must have drifted off at some stage because he was woken by a knocking on his door. "Come in," he called. He realised that he could see across the room so guessed that it was just on dawn.

The door opened and Jane, one of the land girls, stuck her head around the corner.

"Sorry to wake you Mike, but you had better come and look at this."

"OK, just a minute," he replied. Jane closed the door behind her.

'Must be important for her to wake me' he thought to himself. He quickly dressed. "Man its cold," he said out loud as he opened his bedroom door. Jane was waiting in the hall, and led him to the front door. As he came up beside her, she gave him a quick look, and then opened it.

The sight that greeted him caused him to take a step back. The whole doorway was blocked full of snow.

"That's impossible!" he exclaimed. Then he noticed that the top was almost translucent. He pushed against it and it collapsed outwards. Mike looked around the room and laid eyes on the coal shovel. He picked it up and started to dig away at the snow. After only a few minutes it became clear that the apparent extreme depth was only caused by the slight wind piling it up as a tall thin layer, but it was also soon obvious that the real depth was over four feet. By this time the whole family was up and they stared at the drifts spreading out from the house.

"This is serious," Fred finally said as he tried to push his way out through the snow. "This is worse than the 1918 storm."

"Both the power and phone are out too, and the pipes are frozen," Mary added as she came across the lounge from the kitchen.

"Well let's start digging a path to the woodshed and the barn. At least we can have a fire, milk and fresh eggs, provided they are not already frozen," Mike replied as cheerily as he could. "What about Timothy and Susan, aren't they due in tonight?"

"They will be stuck in Christchurch for sure, I wouldn't worry about them, they are the ones who will be worried about us," said Fred, but Mike detected a tinge of concern in his voice.

"I guess so, but we could do with their help right now," Mike sighed as he turned and confronted the wall of snow before him.

It took three days before the snow had melted enough to get in or out even on horseback, but as soon as he was able, Mike headed for Springfield to find Timothy and Susan. He first checked the Railway Station. He expected that the train had not got through from Christchurch and wondered when it would be arriving. What they told him however sent a chill up his spine. Today's train was cancelled the same as the day before, but on the night of the storm it had got through, and Timothy and Susan had been on it. Surely they would hold up in one of the towns hotels reasoned Mike, and he started his hunt for them.

For over four hours he searched. Firstly the hotels, then the lodging houses and finally he rode around the streets calling their names; he found nothing.

Full of dread and worry he started his way back to the farm. He prayed that if they had started the journey back, they had taken refuge in at a farm. If not then their bodies would not be found until the snow thawed. A lump formed in his throat at the thought.

He was nearly halfway back to the farm, when he thought he heard a shout. Mike stopped and scanned the area, but could see nothing. He started to move off again. The sound was very faint, but it was a call of "Help." Again he scanned the snow-covered fields. No fences could be seen although he knew they must be there, but they were covered by a foot of snow, in places even more. Then a slight movement caught the corner of his eye. At first he did not even recognise it as a building, being as it was at the far end of a long paddock, and almost totally buried in snow. But as he looked more carefully he saw the top of a person above the snow, standing in the doorway waving. They were too far away to identify them, but they were obviously in trouble, and as per the unwritten code of the country farmer, when someone is in need you try and help them. Mike's first problem was to find the gate into the paddock. He searched the buried fence line, following the dip in the snow where it had sunk into the drains, and the extra high ridge caused by the hidden fence itself. Finally he saw a rise and guessed it might be an entrance. He carefully nudged his horse up to it and scraped away at the snow, it revealed the top of a wooden gate. Mike climbed off the horse into waist deep snow, and began digging it away from the gate with his gloved hands.

He had been at it for about twenty minutes when a voice from behind asked, "Need any help?"

It was Ted Forrester his neighbour. "Yea somebody is calling for help from the old shed over the far side, give us a hand." Even with the two of them, it only took another twenty minutes to get the gate to a point where they could get the horses through. To try and walk across without snowshoes or skis would be pointless. The snow was far too soft and they would be exhausted before they reached halfway. They remounted their steeds and let them slowly make their own way through the drifts. It took another thirty minutes to get within talking distance of the shed.

"Anybody there?" Mike called out.

"Mike, Mike is that you?"

"Timothy?" His face appeared at the door.

"Mike, Thank goodness, I thought we were all gonna's. Susan is only barely conscious with the cold and the old man I think has frostbite in his toes."

"Ted, go and get help fast, I'll try and keep them alive." He waited until Ted had left.

"What the hell are you doing out here in this weather?" Mike demanded.

"Well we got in a day early, and this man offered to drive us up in his dray. When we left the weather wasn't too bad, but suddenly it just descended on us. Luckily he knew this shed was here and we just headed across the paddock in a whiteout. Even more luckily we found it."

"Cuddle in behind Susan." Mike dragged the now unconscious man over to them and they all lay like sardines sharing as much body heat as they could.

It was over an hour later he guessed when he heard voices outside. Mike got up and looked out. About 20 men were coming across the paddock, some with shovels, some with horses, and at a least four sleds. Mike helped them get Timothy, Susan and the old man on the sleds and then mounted his own horse. He looked around. The top of the dray was now sticking out of the melting snow. He looked about for a horse but saw none. Then on the sheltered side of the shed he saw a lump in the snow. "Poor creature," he said to Ted, "Didn't stand a chance."

Let's just be thankful there isn't three more beside it" Ted replied. The two men looked at each other in silence; then both headed for the gate.

By nightfall the rescued three were in hospital. Timothy and Susan bounced back quickly and returned to the farm the next day. The old man however, lost five of his toes to gangrene, and a week later died.

Many farmers lost substantial quantities of stock that winter. The Standish estate only lost ninety head thanks to their action of bringing in the ones they could, and the fact the paddocks had shelter trees. Christchurch City itself came to a virtual standstill with up to 18 inches of snow lying on city streets. The storm of 1945 would go down as one of the worst in the region.

Life on the farm returned to normal. A few times Timothy tried to coax Mike into finding a girl of his own, but he always seemed to manage to find an excuse, so Timothy did not push the matter too hard.

Timothy was finding work difficult with only one arm, but was able to do jobs like mustering and feeding out from the trailer, and generally being a third arm for Mike when he needed it.

Susan was a great help, to all of them. Mike was concerned that because she did all the cooking and housework she might have felt like a slave to them, but she assured him that it was what she would do for her husband anyway, and he was just another member of her family.

Two years later on the 3rd September 1949, the Standish household increased by one with the birth of Tracy.

This was a whole new experience for Mike as well as for Timothy and Susan. Having a baby underfoot turned the normally orderly routine of the farm into utter chaos. Still it kept him from dwelling too much on his past, when he had a little future right in front of him. He made the perfect Uncle, always there for support, and he was a built in baby sitter. Tracy grew in size and personality. She was a tomboy with a huge heart, tending the newborn animals, caring for the sick ones, and generally got in the way. It was however in 1955 at the age of only six, her true personality came out.

It was about 5am when a knock sounded on his door.

"Come in," he muttered groggily, looking at his bedside clock. 'Something is wrong with one of the animals,' he suspected.

He winced as the light turned on, and he saw it was Timothy, but it was the look on his face that told him this was much worse.

He came over and sat on the side of the bed. "I sorry Mike. Your Mums just died."

Fred took it very hard, and Mike insisted that he move in with him on the farm. The whole tight knit family was devastated.

It took a few days before Susan realised what was going on. Tracy at first just appeared lost, going from person to person and sitting with them for up to half an hour before moving on to the next. She spent however the most time with Fred, just sitting. Susan watched her for a while wondering how she was going to help her daughter get over her apparent sadness, when she realised that Tracy was not sad. From time to time, she would go to her room and play happily with her toys. When they finally asked her why she was doing the rounds, she just said; "Everyone seems so lonely, I just want to keep them company."

Within hours of this revelation becoming common knowledge, everyone had cheered up especially Fred who found he had a new friend in his life.

It was only a year later though and the family was dealt yet another blow, when Stephen passed away at the age of seventy. The Standish farm was now becoming a little crowded, so it was decided that Fred would move in with Carol in Christchurch. Each had their own room, and lived separate lives, but could give each other company and support if needed. The alternative was to put one or both in a rest home, and nobody wanted that. This arrangement initially did raise a few eyebrows in the neighbourhood, but with Fred being seventy one and Carol sixty eight, the rest of the family did not anticipate any 'hanky-panky', and if they did, who would really care. The arrangement worked well until in January 1959, Fred died. Tracy by now was ten, and Mike forty. Mike especially was affected, but once again despite her own grief, Tracy spent a lot of time just being with him.

They brought Carol back to live at the farm, but by now she was showing signs of Alzheimer's. Panic erupted in the Standish household in June the following year when one morning Carol went missing. At first they thought that she had just gone for a short stroll, which she often did, but when she had not returned by lunchtime, they decided to go and look for her. Timothy and a couple of farm hands covered the roads; Susan phoned all the neighbours, while Mike and Tracy searched the farm and surrounds. At three in the afternoon they called the Police, and a search team was assembled, but by now it was nearly dark, and it was very cold. They combed the area until eight, when they had to call it off for the night, to resume again at first light. Everyone held grave fears for her safety as it was not known what she was wearing and even a single night in the open would most likely be fatal.

It was about ten in the evening when the phone rang. A neighbour who had been out all day called to say that he had heard she was missing. He had picked her up walking along the road, and at her request dropped her off at the Springfield railway station.

The Police immediately got in touch with the stationmaster who in turn contacted the person who was selling tickets that day; and found out she had taken the train to Christchurch. Mike guessed she might be heading back to her old home, which was shortly confirmed when at 1 am the Police in Christchurch were called to her old address to pick up a strange elderly woman who was arguing with the owners telling them to get out of her house. They brought her back to the farm but it soon became obvious that she needed nursing care in a secure facility, so six months later, to everybody's agreement but dismay, they put her into a nursing home.

Four more years went by without incident. Tracy was developing into a very attractive young girl, and had many admirers, confirmed by a constant stream of phone calls. But she was always in control of her situation, and never led them on. Consequently she also lost a lot of them; especially when they found out she was not going to give them what they wanted.

Mike watched her grow up. He loved and trusted her, so when she began to ask questions about events in his life, he felt safe in telling her all about the incident in the tunnel. He confided in her more that anyone else, telling her the whole story of the valley and of Paula, and more than anyone else she seemed to grasp the concept and depth of feeling he had for this woman who he had never met except in an illusion. Mike had seldom spoken to anyone since he had accepted that the events of those nine days were in his head, but she understood that by letting Mike talk about it, it was helping him with his loss.

CHAPTER 23

It was on one fine Saturday summer's evening, after Mike had been helping Timothy laying a new path out to the clothes line that Tracy came and sat down beside him.

"Have you ever met Paula's parents?"

The question came out of nowhere, and took him back a little.

"No I haven't."

"Why not?"

"Well it would be a little difficult don't you think?"

"Why?"

"I can just imagine walking up to them and saying, Hi my name is Mike and I had an imaginary love affair with your daughter 2 years after she died."

"Hummf." She thought for a minute. "Well you could say you had a love affair just before she went missing… And that she was tramping on your farm."

"Well apart from the fact I would be lying, I don't know where they live, or if they are even alive. Anyway, why the interest?"

"Aren't you curious about her life, where she lived, what her parents were like?"

"Well yes of course, but ..."

"So find out." Tracy stated, "I'd love to know."

"Tracy you're sixteen, you love to know everything."

"Yep, especially about romantic love affairs, steeped in mystery like yours, and you know how I love mysteries."

"Oh there's no mystery about mine," Mike laughed. "Just a bang on the head and you're off in fairyland for a few days … months … years."

"Uncle, I'm serious. When was her birthday?"

"I don't know," Mike had to admit.

"See, if you met them you could find out and celebrate it."

Mike sighed. "I'll think about."

Tracy passed her dad as she was about to go into her room.

"Dad, I've just been talking to Uncle Mike about Paula. I can't remember her surname. Can you remember what it was?"

Timothy thought for a moment "Hamil... no Henderson."

"Thanks dad," and she quickly disappeared.

Timothy stared at the closed door and shook his head. "Teenagers; I thought us oldies had bad memories," he muttered to himself as he went in search of Mike.

"There you are," and handed him a cold beer. "Tracy's been bugging you?"

Mike smiled and took a long drink from the bottle.

"She reckons I should find Paula's parents."

"That's not really practical is it?"

"Not unless I tell a couple of fibs, still it would be interesting."

Neither of them noticed the curtain in Tracy's room move as she slipped away from the slightly open window.

It was Tracy's good marks that finally unravelled her well-conceived little plan. The class had been given an assignment on genealogy. Tracy had of course set about locating the parents of Paula, with remarkable success. She had gone through all the phone books looking for Henderson's, and there had been quite a few. Next she had, through the school, contacted Births, Deaths and Marriages and located a Paula Henderson that had died in 1937. Then she had checked all the death notices and found the correct one, and then crossed referenced the information between that and the phone listings. It had been a long shot, but she had the answer. The teacher had been so impressed at her logic and tenacity, that she had given her top marks, and sent home a letter to her parents to acknowledge the fact.

Timothy and Susan were delighted and wanted to see the work she had done. They were not so pleased at the subject.

Mike looked up from watching the news and saw the contrite little group assembled at the lounge door.

"This does not look good," he said eyeing them up suspiciously.

"Tracy has something to tell you," Timothy prompted.

"I'm sorry Uncle Mike, I didn't mean any harm."

Mike knew that she did not have a nasty bone in her body and that what ever she had done, she probably hadn't meant to. He looked at her as sternly as he could. "Well?"

She looked down at the ground.

"Tracy, tell Mike what you have done," Susan said quietly behind her.

"Uncle Mike, I've found Paula's parents."

"Mike," Susan cut in quickly. "I have the details on this piece of paper. I will give it to you if you wish, or I will destroy it. Whatever you want."

Mike was genuinely shocked. That was definitely not what he was expecting.

He looked at Tracy as a tear ran down her cheek.

"You know, if you had asked me if you could do it, I would probably have said no." He looked at Susan. "What do you think?" He asked.

"I guess its one of those things where, if you don't do it you will never know, and it will probably nag you for the rest of your life. But it's entirely up to you."

"How did you find it?"

"I did it as a special assignment at school," Tracy answered trying hard not to sob.

"Did you get good marks?"

Tracy looked her mum.

"Top of the class, and with a special mention. That's how we found out," Susan replied for her.

"Bring it here." Mike beckoned Tracy over.

She stood beside him, and he looked up into her young pretty face. She definitely had her mother's looks he mused as she looked back at him with big puppy eyes, wet and pleading.

"Sometimes you just have to follow your instincts, and just be prepared to take the consequences whatever they are." He sighed. "No matter what you may have been told. I guess this may be one of those times."

"So what should be a fitting punishment then?" Susan asked.

Mike looked at them each in turn considering, and then returned his gaze to Tracy.

"Can we really punish her for getting top of the class, do you think?"

He was suddenly embraced with two arms and she kissed him on the cheek. "I love you Uncle Mike."

She stood up with a big grin that soon faded as she saw the 'Don't push it girl' look from Timothy.

Quickly she walked across the room, slipped between her parents, and out the door.

Timothy put his hand on Susan's back and turned to go. "You big softy," was all he said over his shoulder as he left the room. Mike sat back in the chair running his fingers around the edge of the folded paper for a good half hour. He knew as soon as he laid eyes on that address he would have to visit them.

Susan sat beside him on the arm of the chair.

"Are you alright? She should not have done that. I'm sorry."

Mike put his hand on hers. "She is a very caring, loving girl. I know she was doing what she thought was best, and maybe it is. I would never have done it myself, although I have thought I would have liked to have met them many times. Now I can. That is if I can muster up the courage."

Mike looked down at the paper and taking a deep breath opened it.

"Andrew and Teresa Henderson, 117 Blake St Blenheim."

"When do you think you will go?" Susan asked.

"Let me get a believable story together. Maybe next week."

"Do you want to drive up? Or would you want, Timothy or me to take you?"

"No I won't drive. I'll take the train up. I can stay a day in Christchurch, and then go up to Blenheim. Stay a couple of nights and come back. It will do me good to get away for a few days. Timothy can run things here."

"OK, and dinners on the table in ten minutes."

CHAPTER 24

Monday morning Susan drove Mike to the station at Springfield, a town of some 500 people and 43 miles from Christchurch. Springfield was the gateway to the Southern Alps. From here the railway wound its way up through the mountains past Mike's farm, to Arthur's Pass. However today he would be travelling about 1 1/2 hours through the mainly flat fields of the Canterbury Plains in the other direction.

A whistle announced the arrival of the train. Mike handed his suitcase to the porter and then found his carriage. He located his seat and settled in for the journey.

He booked into a small hotel for the night near the Railway station for ease of catching the early morning train to Picton. He thought of calling Paula's parents and warning them of his arrival, but if they did not understand and said no, it would be difficult to arrange any further contact. Better just to arrive in person, unannounced.

He had a quick breakfast of eggs and sausages, washed down with an overly strong and almost unpalatably bitter coffee, and made his way to the station. It was always a pleasant trip up the South Island Main Trunk. The railway hugged the coast for a lot of the way and the view was normally spectacular. On this day however, it was raining and overcast. They stopped for a break at Kaikoura and then carried on until they reach Blenheim around 3pm. Mike collected his luggage and hailed a taxi to take him to his hotel.

Blenheim, with a population of around 12,000, was central to a major sheep-farming region, and was the principal commercial town and administrative centre for the greater part of Marlborough. The hotel was of a high standard for a provincial town. He checked in, and after depositing his belongings, wandered out into the street. He picked up a bus timetable and map then returned to his room to work out the route and times. Then after watching the Television for a while, he sat back and read a book until nearly 10pm.

He had a fitful night's sleep, what with an unfamiliar bed and the worry of what the coming day was to bring, so by morning was starting to wish he had never come.

After breakfast he found the appropriate bus stop, and within 20 minutes was in Paula's street. He watched the numbers climb. "Next stop please," he said to the driver.

Mike sat in a bus shelter almost directly across the road from the little white house for nearly ten minutes.

It was not a big place, just an average three bedroom home on a quarter acre section. A white picket fence across the front, contained a row of nicely pruned rose bushes. 'It must look a picture in summer,' he thought. A brick path led in a curve, carving a red sweep through the freshly mowed grass from the gate to the steps leading up onto the veranda.

Taking a deep breath he crossed the road and opened the gate.

He hesitated, took another deep breath and knocked on the door. Soon he saw a figure slowly moving through the mottled pattern of the stained glass; then the door opened. An elderly woman stood there, one hand on her walking stick.

"Yes, can I help you?" she asked.

Mike cleared his throat.

"Mrs Henderson?"

"Yes that's right."

"I know you don't know me, but my name is Mike Standish, and I used to know your daughter Paula."

She eyed him up and down for a minute.

"Who is it dear?" A grey haired thin gentleman appeared in the hallway.

"A man who says he used to know Paula."

"What do you want?" she asked a little hesitantly.

"I own the farm above the area where she went missing, and she would sometimes talk with me when she went tramping. I was just in town here and thought I would look you up."

She stood and looked at him, a kind of quizzical "so what," expression on her face.

Mike was feeling very awkward and starting to regret this. "Well, she used to talk a lot about you and as I am probably one of the last people to see her, ahhh ummm …alive."

"Oh well come in for a minute," she said, then turned and walked down the hall. Mike slipped off his shoes and closed the door, then followed her into the living room.

"Sit down young man," and she indicated the couch to the side of the fireplace.

It was a homely room. The fireplace was on the end of the building with a small window each side. To the roadside was a set of French doors that led out onto the veranda. Two well padded and well worn, but not in any way tatty armchairs sat side by side across the corner facing him. In the middle of the room was a low antique coffee table. To the other side of him was an ornate bookcase, crammed with books of all shapes and sizes. Between the fireplace and the French doors stood a beautiful Kauri china cabinet, filled with a wide variety of exquisite plates and figurines. Pictures covered the wall, but what drew him out of his chair was a framed colour photo on the mantle piece. Obviously professionally taken, it was a beautiful head and shoulders portrait of

180

Paula. As he stood and looked at it, a lump rose in his throat and he had a hard fight to hold back the tears that he could already feel welling up in him.

"So you new Paula you say," the old man asked after watching him for a moment.

"Yes I did, quite well; we had … ahh … some long talks." Mike sat back down.

"Do you know anything more about her disappearance?" the old lady asked. That question nearly threw him. This was much harder that he had imagined.

"No, I can't say for sure what has happened to her." This he knew was the truth.

"I know this may seem a bit rude of me," he looked back up at the mantle piece, "but would you have a picture of her I could have."

The old couple looked at each other, then her mother shrugged, "I guess so, but why would you want one?"

"I'll go and have a look," her father said, and eased himself out of his chair.

"I was going through an album of all the people I know and have met over the years, and found that I had not taken one of her, and I would like something to look at in later years."

The old man returned with a cardboard box and the pair of them rummaged through what was obviously and pile of photos. They stopped at one. "Will this do?" Mike stood up and walked across to them. It was a reasonable quality picture, not as good as the one on the mantle piece, but much better than the sketch from the poster, which was all he had up till now.

"That will be fine, I'm very grateful for your time, and this," he said holding up the photo. "I shan't keep you any longer."

They both stood up. Mike walked back to the mantle piece for one last look. She looked so happy, peaceful, almost laughing. He could imagine the place with her in it. It would have seldom been quiet. "She was a sweet gentle girl," he said keeping his now damp eyes on the picture, not daring to turn around.

"Yes she was very special," he heard her mother say.

"I love the way she wrinkled her nose," he said more to himself, than to the others.

He gave the photo one long last look and sighed; then he turned to go.

Her husband was helping his wife back into her seat. Both had a strange look on their face.

"Oh my, Oh my dear boy," She said as she put her hand to her chest.

"Are you alright?" he asked fearing that his presence had been too much for her. "I had better go."

"No, no, stay please, she quickly replied. "Andrew, get the boy a drink, tea, coffee, and some of that chocolate cake, the one in the green tin." She indicated for him to sit.

"What would you like?"

"Coffee please," Mike stammered. 'What the hell just happened,' he thought, stunned at the sudden change.

"Jug's on." Her husband returned with a tin, three plates and a knife. He opened it and took out the cake, putting it on the lid to cut it.

"You're not telling us the whole truth, are you my boy?" Her mother suddenly said.

A knot formed in Mike's stomach, he had been caught out in his deception. He frantically thought back on what could have given him away. 'Oh no, maybe they know all about me and my delusions. Has she not ever tramped there before, I'm sure she said she had.'

No, he decided, they had been on to him from the beginning. How could he have possibly thought that someone this close to her would not have heard about the lunatic from the tunnel who had raved on about meeting Paula, even though it was all those years ago.

"What do you mean?" he managed to say a little shakily.

"You knew her a lot better than you are making out; in fact you were very close."

He felt the tears starting to well up in his eyes. These were her parents, the ones closest to her. They should by now have been his in-laws. 'No that's not possible, it's only an illusion, stop mixing it up with reality' he reminded himself harshly. But the hurt was still so real. His shoulders sank and he slumped back on the couch.

"Did you love her?" That question shook him to the core.

"Yes." Was all he could muster to say, feeling totally defeated.

"She must have loved you very much too. It's funny she never mentioned you. Ahh, but that was Paula. One day she would have stridden in here, larger than life, and introduced you are her fiancé."

Mike swallowed. He knew that is probably what would have happened.

"Tell us about yourself and how you got to know her."

Now Mike really knew he was in a difficult situation. Could he actually tell them that her daughter had been alive, held captive? Could he say that he had fallen in love with her in … in a delusion?

Suddenly Tracy's words came back to him. "Make the dream happen on your farm and not in the valley, that's all you have to change; the location."

Mike told them about his family, how he had supposedly met her while tramping behind the farm.

He told her of horse riding and walking by the river, of summer nights and happy times.

"Were you going to get married?"

Mike gave a deep sigh, and for several moments stared at the floor. Then he slowly raised his head to look at them. "I proposed just before ... before she disappeared. We were going to tell everybody when she got back."

They chatted a bit more about things in general, finally Mike stood up. "I really must go now, thank you so much for talking with me and for the photo."

"Ah yes, just a minute." And the old lady shuffled out of the room.

She soon returned. "Give me back that old thing, have this one instead."

She handed Mike a framed colour photo, it was the same as the one on the mantle piece. "We got these done at her last birthday. Under the circumstances I think you should have one too."

That was the last straw for him as he put his arms around her and wept.

"Thank you again so much Mr and Mrs Henderson," he finally said. "It has meant so much to me."

"Please call us Andrew and Teresa, and please do keep in touch. After all you are almost family. In fact as far as I am concerned, you are family. Paula did not have a lot of friends, and hardly any male friends, so I guess you are the son-in-law we almost had."

"I will, I promise," Mike replied, and he meant it. He felt he owed it to Paula, even if she was an illusion, because for him, she was real. He was just about to turn and step across the porch, when he stopped.

"Mrs. Hend... I mean Teresa, I don't mean to be rude, but please answer me this. When I arrived you were quite cool with me, and rightly so; then something changed. I don't understand. How could you possibly know we loved each other?"

"It was you who told me." Mike looked at her puzzled. Teresa continued. "You said she wrinkled her nose at you. That was a nervous trait of hers that only manifested itself when she was showing love to someone. Like when she gave us presents at Christmas or birthdays, or that time I was in hospital," she said looking at Andrew. He nodded. "And she brought me that huge bouquet of flowers. For you to have seen that, and seen it enough for you to pick up on it, she must have really loved you. I thought she had never done it to anybody else but us, until now.

It was the persistent knocking that brought him back to reality. He looked around trying to work out where he was. The knock sounded again. "Mr Standish, Mr Standish, Room Service. Are you alright?"

Mike got off the bed, and opened the door. A porter stood there with a trolley on which stood two trays of food covered by a round metal lid.

"Mr Standish, I was getting worried."

"Why, can I help?"

"Your dinner Sir."

Mike looked at him blankly.

"You ordered it when you came in. Remember I asked you in the foyer, at the concierge? You looked a little upset so I asked if you wanted dinner in your room."

"Oh yes thanks," Mike replied still having no recollection of the encounter.

The man put it on the table and went to the door. "Goodnight Mr Standish," he said as started to go out.

"Night; what is the time?"

"It's 9.30 in the evening. Is there anything I can do for you?"

"No that's all. Thank you." The door closed.

Mike sat down on the corner of his bed. He had no idea how he had even got back from the Henderson's or anything else for that matter since he had heard those words.

He thought back all those years. What had the psychiatrist said? "It is always going to be an illusion until you have irrefutable proof."

He had checked out all the details. Paula, the Kennards, even the valley, though that was still open to debate. All had a possible explanation. Everything pointed to a tortured mind that had survived by inventing an imaginary world, and filling it with snippets of fact to create a believable story.

Now; now that was turned completely upside down. All the years of research; all the possible explanations; shattered by a simple of-the-cuff statement.

"She wrinkled her nose." Mike knew it was that irrefutable proof.

He had realised it, the moment he heard Teresa's words. There was NO way he could have known that fact unless he really had known her in person, but not just known her; loved her; and received that love back in return.

He suddenly felt sick in his stomach. He had at last found the truth, but in doing so had just lost his peace, the illusion that protected him, and his fiancé. He rushed to the toilet and vomited.

CHAPTER 25

It was Susan and Tracy who came and picked him up. The hotel had rung them saying that Mike was still in his room, that he should have checked out and that they thought he was very distressed.

Tracy of course was very worried, after all it had been her idea to go and see them. Something had obviously happened and she felt very guilty.

They arrived late in the afternoon in Blenheim, and located the hotel. The clerk at the concierge saw her arrive. 'What a stunner, and her daughter is just as good looking' he thought as they approach.

"Hello, I'm Susan Standish; I believe Mike Standish is staying here."

"Yes he is; shall I call him?"

"What room is he in?" Susan asked.

"202 up the stairs."

"Good, then give me a key."

"I'm sorry madam but I can't do that."

"You called me up here to help, now GIVE … ME … THE … KEY!"

He dropped it into her hand, though she was not sure if it was through fear, or because he was besotted with her looks or both. Either way she had it.

"Thank you," she said in her normal quiet sweet voice, and headed for the stairs.

"Here it is," Tracy called.

Susan did not bother to knock; she just unlocked it and barged in. Mike was lying on the bed fully clothed. A plate of cold food still sat on the table.

"Uncle Mike, Uncle Mike are you OK?" Tracy ran around to face him.

Susan sat on the side of the bed. "Mike what has happened?"

He slowly raised himself up to sitting position. To Susan he looked as if he had aged fifty years. He was unshaven and grey, a look of total devastation masked his face.

"Is he alright?" The clerk stood at the door.

"Get us three coffees please," Susan answered without looking up.

"Ah well there is a little matter of the bill, you see…"

"I will fix all that up tomorrow. Oh, and we are all staying here in this room tonight, and we will have dinner. Do you have a roast on the menu? Good. Three meals and desert please, at 7pm. Thank you, that's all."

The clerk stood staring at her for a moment, then with a voice that sounded only a step away from terrified replied, "yes madam." Quickly he closed the door and disappeared.

Mike looked at her. "Paula existed."

Susan looked at him puzzled. "We know that," she said in a voice that was as much a question as a statement.

"I mean I was with her in the valley."

Tracy and Susan exchanged glances.

"I found that irrefutable evidence."

They sat up most of the evening. Mike told them all that had happened. Susan made sure that he ate and drank, and queried him often about what had been said.

About 11pm she left him dressed and pulled a sheet over him, then climbed in beside him herself. Tracy curled up on the couch. She looked at her daughter across the room. She appeared drawn and tired, and had been unusually quiet.

It had been a tough day for her. She had tried to put her off coming on the trip, but Tracy had insisted. 'She is as stubborn as I am when I get my mind set on something'. She smiled 'And just like me, she usually achieves what she sets out to accomplish.'

Susan rang for room service to bring up a breakfast for them all around 8am, and after paying the bill, she bundled them all in the car and headed back to the farm.

It was a quiet trip back. The usually exuberant Tracy sat staring out the window most of the time. Mike seemed also to be lost in a thought filled world of his own. They stopped at Kaikoura for lunch, and then took the inland road through Rangiora and Oxford to join the West Coast Road at Waddington. It was nearly dark when they got back to the farm.

Both Mike and Tracy went to bed early. Susan sat up with Stephen and told him all that had happened.

The next morning Mike felt angry, betrayed. He had been led all this time to believe that his relationship with Paula was a figment of a tortured mind.

How could Tony have been so wrong? He needed to have this out, to put him straight.

Mike dialled the number.

"Christchurch Mental Health Unit," a voice answered. "Yes I need to speak with… Never mind I will come and speak to him personally."

Mike crossed the room and into the kitchen. "I'll be back tomorrow," he said as he took his keys off the hook. He had not noticed that Susan had been standing in the doorway listening.

"You are NOT driving to Christchurch!"

Susan stood firmly in front of him. "I will take you tomorrow morning, now give me those keys."

Mike glared back at her, but there was no change in her stance. Instead she thrust out her hand towards him. He looked her in the eyes. They were hard with determination, but also full of love and concern. Beautiful and deceptively fragile she appeared, but he was quite sure that if he tried to drive off she would lay down in front of his car if she needed to, to stop him. There was no further argument. He dropped the keys into her hand and stalked back to his bedroom.

The next day, true to her word, they departed for Christchurch.

Susan knew that this was very important to him, and she was going to see him through it. But she was also scared for him. She had learned of his previous mental state and although she had no concern for herself, she instinctively felt that he should not be alone for his own safety.

They said little on the trip in and it was just after lunch that they pulled up in the hospital car park. Mike knew where he was going; he had met Tony here many times before, but not for several years. He approached reception.

"I need to see Tony Bloomfield urgently," he stated to the lady behind the counter.

She stared at him for a moment obviously unsure of what to do.

"Tony Bloomfield. I used to be a patient of his, and I need to talk to him immediately," he repeated a little more agitatedly.

"Ahh umm just wait here a moment please." She hurried into an adjacent office.

Mike paced up and down the waiting room occasionally looking at the people sitting there. A few looked back; some just stared at the floor. A young man sat in the corner having an imaginary conversation with someone invisible to all but himself. Mike stopped and watched him. He had thought that he had been having conversations with an imaginary person. His person had now become real.

"Excuse me," a voice asked.

It was the receptionist. "Can I have your name please?"

Even through his anger, Mike could detect something was not quite right. Was he refusing to see him? Maybe he no longer worked here. Then he would find out where he was and go to him there.

"Mike Standish. He WILL see me."

The woman hastily disappeared.

Mike turned to look at Susan. She returned his gaze, showing no obvious emotion, but indicated that he should sit beside her. Silently Mike complied.

It was not long before a man who he had not seen before appeared with the receptionist, and she pointed Mike out to him. Mike stood up and met him half way across the floor. Uninvited Susan stood up also and walked up beside him.

"Mr Standish?"

"Yes. I want to see Tony Bloomfield, and if he is not here I want to know where he is. I need to talk with him, and I won't be fobbed off."

The man sighed. "Come with me." he said and led them through a side door and down a short corridor to a small consultation room.

Mr Standish, "My name is Doctor Cropper; I am the head Psychiatrist here."

"I need to talk to Tony," insisted Mike.

The man looked at Mike for a few seconds then let out his breath.

"You have not seen him for a while."

"No, but if I ever needed to talk to him he said he would be there for me. I need to talk to him now!"

"There is no easy way to put this. Tony went to Vietnam last year with a civilian surgical team to get hands on assessment of front line mental heath problems. He was killed by a sniper two days before he was due to return. I'm sorry."

Mike felt his world start to crumble. He stood up totally lost, not knowing what to do, or say. Two arms wrapped around him and he grabbed hold of Susan, holding her tight against him, and he cried.

"I will send someone out to see you tomorrow to assess your needs, but until then take these, they may help." He put a jar of pills in Mike's hand. Mike just nodded and Susan helped him back to the car. They drove home in silence. Mike found he was no longer angry, but now he was almost back where he started, and Susan was desperately worried that he would sink into severe depression. Stephen came out and met them at the door of the car.

"We have a problem," he said.

"So do we." Susan cut in. "Tony died in Vietnam last year, and Mike is really down."

"He's not the only one. Tracy hasn't eaten since you left and won't come out of her room."

"Why not?"

"She is blaming herself for what has happened to Mike, you had better see what you can do."

Neither had noticed Mike get out of the car.

"No; let me go to her. I know she will talk to me, and right now I think we need each other. I'm not going to let her take the blame for me. It's our problem and we need to sort it for both our sakes."

Susan looked at Stephen. He nodded. She put her hands on Mikes arm as he moved to go inside. He stopped and gave her a weak smile. She let him pull away realising that the self-therapy was already working.

"He's right. They both need to get better for the sake of the other. Neither is going to let the other down, they have no choice but to rise up."

"Yep, they are both pretty stubborn." Stephen replied, as they went back inside.

Mike knocked on Tracy's door.

There was no response.

He knocked harder

"Go away!" came from inside.

"I'm not going anywhere." Mike replied.

For a moment there was silence, then he heard the door unlock.

She pulled it open and stood in the frame.

For over a minute they just stood looking at each other, then, Mike took her by the hands and guided her backwards into the room. They sat together on the side of the bed without a word; suddenly Tracy threw her arms around him.

"I'm sorry Uncle Mike, it's all my fault, I should never have done it. Now I have hurt you, I'm so sorry." She pushed herself back and looked at him, tears streaming down her face. Mike just gave her a smile and pulled her back into his arms and they cried together.

Susan quietly slipped away from where she had stood close to the open door, and returned to the lounge. Stephen looked up worriedly as she came in. Silently she closed the hall door behind her before speaking.

"They will be just fine. Just give them whatever space they need. Don't try and help, just treat them as if everything is normal." They sat for a while wondering what normal meant.

Stephen was about to say something when they heard the door handle rattle.

Mike came in followed by Tracy his arm around her shoulder.

"We are just going outside to get some air," he said as they shuffled passed. Tracy gave them a slight smile. "I'm sorry," she said quietly.

"That's OK darling," Susan replied.

They watch them go out the door.

"I wish she would eat something," Stephen said almost to himself.

"She will eat when she is ready, but right now she needs some special comfort that we cannot give her. However, boy will she eat when she does feel like it. I think I will make some chicken nibbles and put them in the refrigerator."

Mike and Tracy sat on the bench seat overlooking the valley and the railway.

"I." "We." they both said together.

"You first," Mike said to her.

"I never wanted to hurt you; I thought it would be nice for you to know more about her. It's all turned out so wrong."

"Tracy, it's not your fault. I made the decision to go, not you. But you gave me something very precious."

She looked up at him from where she sat, her head hung and her hands between her knees.

"You gave me the truth. Something I have searched for since my accident. But I settled for something less. Sometimes the truth hurts. Sometimes you wish you never knew it. Sometimes it's easier to live with a lie, but the truth is still the truth, and now I know it, I have to live with it. And so do you."

They sat in silence for many minutes, each sorting out their inner emotions.

"Mike. Just because you know it is no longer an illusion doesn't change the way you feel about her does it?, I mean she was always real to you anyway, it just proves that the valley exists..." she stopped and looked up the snow capped peaks in the distance..., out there somewhere."

Mike followed her gaze.

'She was right. What had changed? Well for one thing he had gained a pseudo mother and father-in-law.'

Tracy seemed to read his mind. "Are you going to see them again?"

"Yes I think I am ... now, thanks to you. I owe it to Paula to look after them."

"That would be nice," Tracy said in a wistful kind of way.

"And I suppose you would want to come along."

"Only to look after you."

Mike looked at her, she had changed. He suddenly felt that he had started this conversation with a girl and ended it with a young woman.

He held out his hand and she hugged him. "I love you Uncle Mike."

"I love you too Tracy."

"I'm hungry, let's get something to eat."

They walked back to the house with an arm over each others shoulder.

CHAPTER 26

Over the next few years there were many times when Mike and Tracy would discuss things that they would never have discussed with anyone else. They had built a special trust, a closeness that transcended even the difference between them in years. Although she had the usual mother/daughter, daughter/father conversations, she would often talk to Mike about things normally reserved for a close confidant her own age.

Mike travelled to see Paula's parents at least once every two months, and Tracy would often be with him. They both had made a vow to keep the actual circumstances of Mike's affair with Paula a secret, discussing events as if they had eventuated on the farm, not in Kennard's valley. He helped them with any small jobs, and repaired things that needed fixing, and was always there for their birthdays, and Paula's. If he did not make Christmas, then he would be there at New Year.

It was in the winter of 1968 that Teresa, at the age of seventy-six, got a bad cold. That in turn developed into pneumonia. She passed away in November of that year. Mike had discussed everything with Andrew prior to the event and so all went smoothly for the funeral. Mike and Tracy were, of course, there. Mike had been particularly hard hit not having had Paula around, but again he and Tracy, found the needed strength that only they could muster to support each other.

Andrew who was now seventy eight, asked Mike to help him get into a rest home and he and Tracy moved him in and arranged the sale of the house.

Tracy got a job at the local Post Office in Springfield, and was soon assistant Post Mistress.

By 1969 Tracy had developed into a stunning twenty-year-old confident woman. Men would walk into power poles and trip over billboards as she passed by. But like her Mother she was no flirt or easy catch. She knew what she wanted in a man and when she saw it, she would go after him, and she would dictate the terms of the relationship. A couple of lads had tried to land her, but if they took her for a bimbo, they were sorely mistaken. She very soon determined that they would not give her what she wanted in a marriage, and told them so.

Mike knew however. It had been one of those in depth conversations that would make most older men blush, and fathers go grey. They had discussed every aspect of what women needed, what men needed and what made for a good relationship. They looked at her mother's marriage with Stephen and decided it was pretty close to 'as good as it got', and based their thoughts around that. Mike knew that whomever she chose would be a lucky man, as long as he treated her right. 'And he had better' thought Mike 'or he will answer to me.'

Not long after her twenty-first however she asked the family if she could bring home a friend that she had met in high school. He had been in Auckland serving an apprenticeship as a fitter in the Railway workshops, and had now returned home to look for work in the South Island. They had met again in town, and had started having lunch together.

"What's his name?" asked Susan.

"Martin Strathmore."

"Well, well, a Strathmore," Mike commented.

"You know them?" Susan answered.

"Yes they are one of the Springfield originals like us."

"And?" prompted Susan.

"And?" added Tracy.

Mike sat back, put his hands behind is head, and smiled.

"And … they are one of the Springfield originals. That's all," he replied innocently.

Two sets of eyes levelled at him.

"Like two peas in a pod," he reflected.

Tracy came over and sat on the arm of his chair.

"Uncle Mike," she said sweetly, turning her head to look him in the face, and opening her eyes wide, to give him that puppy dog look. "Tell us what you know," she continued in her innocent quiet voice, "Or I'll break your fingers."

He held up his forefinger, and then quickly retracted the same as she made a grab for it.

"Such a sweet girl," he said looking across at Susan.

"The Strathmore's," she replied, "Give it up."

"Well they are well liked. Cecil has helped me out on several occasions and I him in return. They a reasonably well off I think. He loaned us that tractor last year when ours broke down, remember?"

"Oh yes, them; Cecil and Gwyneth. I only ever knew them by their first names, didn't connect them with the name Strathmore at all. Yes a lovely couple, and I think I knew Martin too, when he was at school."

"Yes. Happy to have him over. Do you want me to make anything special?"

They saw quite a lot of Martin over the next few months. Mike watched with interest the developing relationship. He liked Martin, who by now had taken a job in a small local engineering shop, and did not think the work beneath him coming down from railway locomotives to plows. Tracy too was acting very mature, so he was not surprised when one afternoon she took his hand and said, "Uncle Mike, I want to talk."

They went out to their now special seat for a heart to heart discussion, and, as usual, sat looking out over the mountains.

"What do you think?" she asked.

"I think you have got your hooks well embedded, and you should start reeling him in."

"Uncle Mike!" Tracy started in feigned shock.

She laid her head on his shoulder. "I want you to be with me and Dad on the platform. I want you both to give me away."

"That's a bit unorthodox isn't it?"

"Yes but you are both so special to me. You have been my friend and confidant and like a father to me also. Will you please?"

"Only after I talk with Stephen. If I get the slightest hint that he may be upset, then I will step down. It is his special day too."

Tracy gave him a big hug, and then turned around. She waved behind her. "He said yes," she called excitedly.

Mike looked over his shoulder. Stephen and Susan stood in the doorway. At her prompting they came over.

"She asked you then," Stephen said as he approached.

"I get the feeling I have been set up," Mike replied.

"You have, and I would be honoured to have you on the stage beside me my friend," he replied.

In December 1971, at the Standish Estate, on a specially made stage, just like her Mother, little Tracy Standish became Mrs Tracy Strathmore.

Martin and Tracy rented a little cottage in Springfield, and six months later Martin applied for a job back with the railways in the workshops at Addington. It was only a week or two before he was asked to go in for an interview. Tracy also applied for a transfer to any branch in the Christchurch area, and in no time was accepted as Assistant Manager at a small branch in Riccarton. A few weeks later and both families, the Standish and the Strathmore's were ferrying the young couple's belongings to a comfortable three-bedroom house in Fendalton.

The next year Mike and Tracy had another funeral to attend. This time it was Andrew's. Some of the family came over from Australia to the funeral. Mike had not met any of them. It was quite a shock to all when he found that he was also named in the will and received $150,000 from the estate. He expected to have his share contested, but as he found out at the function that followed, his kindness and attachment to Paula had been transmitted to a much wider audience, and he was instead, given special thanks for all he had done for the family.

Mike humbly accepted the money and promptly gave it to Tracy and Martin despite their protests.

As he put it "I would not even had met them if it wasn't for you and your school assignment." Tracy studied him for a moment then tenderly kissed him on the cheek. She knew that he had got something money could never buy from those resultant years, and how much he had appreciated her loyalty over the years. To refuse would only hurt him.

Thirteen relatively uneventful years drifted past. Tracy and Martin had decided not to have children too early in their life together, but as they approached their mid thirties, Susan had started to drop hints, and some not too subtle, that she might like to become a grandmother one day. So at the age of 35, and to Mike's delight, Tracy became pregnant.

Mike woke to the ringing of the phone.

He groped around for his glasses and noted the time, 3am. "Who the hell is this ringing at this time," he said out loud as he climbed out of bed. He staggered across the room ricocheting off the door jam into the passage wall.

'Why bother,' he muttered as he entered the hall and turned on the light. 'It will have stopped by the time I get there.'

It however did not. "Hello, who's that?" he yelled at the phone before the hand piece had even reached his ear

"Mike its Martin."

Now Mike was quickly starting to focus. Martin did not make a habit of early morning calls unless something was wrong. "What's wrong is everyone OK?" Mike asked annoyance changing to the apprehension obvious in his voice.

"Yes; don't panic. Tracy's waters have broken and the ambulance is taking her up to the hospital."

"She's early isn't she?, is she OK? What about the baby? Why the ambulance?"

"Its fine Mike, don't panic, it's only 4 days early, but I knew you would want to know."

"What hospital?"

"St Georges Maternity."

"I'll meet you there shortly."

"I guess there isn't any point in saying there's no need."

"No!"

"OK I'll see you there." Martin hung up, turned and smiled at his wife. "He's going to spoil her rotten you know," he said.

"I know," Tracy replied, then grimaced as she felt the next contraction coming.

It took him only an hour to reach Christchurch at that time of day, and he went straight into the maternity ward.

"Tracy Standish please," he said to the lady at reception.

"And your name sir?"

"Mike Standish."

"And you are Tracy's …"

"Father." he lied without thinking.

The nurse looked him up and down. "Just a minute please," and she disappeared down the corridor.

She returned a few moments later with Timothy in tow.

"Tracy's father, meet Tracy's father." She stood back and watched.

The two men shook hands then hugged.

"One of you is lying. Who is Tracy's father?"

Both at once they answered in unison. "He is."

"So, which of you is lying."

"I am," came the identical replies.

By now both men were grinning from ear to ear.

"So do I kick both of you out, or let both of you in."

"In." came the united chorus.

"OK, but one of you had better be an Uncle if the Matron comes around."

"I will," replied Mike

"He will," answered Timothy, and they both hastily moved down the corridor before she changed her mind, or they pushed their luck too far.

Timothy led Mike into a room on the right.

As he entered he saw Martin sitting beside Tracy who lay in the bed. Susan stood to one side, and as soon as she saw him, rushed over and gave him a big kiss.

"Welcome in Uncle Mike, come and meet your third cousin Karla."

Martin turned from where he sat with his back to the door and stood as Mike approached and handed him a little bundle of towels.

Mike took them and looked in at the little girl wrapped up in the folds. She stared up at him, trying to focus, and appeared to giggle."

"Just 1/2 an hour old," Tracy said.

He looked down at her lying there and suddenly, just for a split second, he saw Paula looking back at him.

Tracy also caught the wave of emotion on his face.

"Are you OK Uncle Mike?" she asked softly.

He took a deep breath and looked back at the little girl in his arms.

"Yes, I'm fine, just thinking of what could have been."

"I guessed as much. But you have a beautiful grand niece, and I'm sure she will get lots of love from you."

The door opened and in its place stood the matron. "What is going on in here?" she demanded

"Who is the father?"

"Not me," all three men said as one, then all burst into laughter.

"Get out! Get out all of you and let the mother and baby have some rest."

They all traipsed by the bed and gave Tracy a cuddle. Mike deposited the child back into her arms.

They looked at each other, a silent communication between them. Then he kissed her and the baby and stood up. He gave the Matron his best "I am ever so nice," smile as he passed her. She glared back at him. "Men," he heard her say to Tracy, as he wandered down to the waiting room.

In April 1988 Mike called a family conference.

By then he was 69 years old. Timothy was 67 and Tracy 39.

"Does anybody want to take over the running and ownership of the farm," was the burning question.

Timothy was the only one with any farming experience and he was enjoying retirement.

"You are the only one who has kept the place going all these years, it should go to who you choose," Timothy answered.

"I was considering selling it. Except the tunnel corner with the homestead of course. I will keep that to live in."

"And do what?" replied Tracy

"I think I am ready to retire also."

"Hooray," shouted Susan. "It's about time you took it easy."

Mike continued. "If it's alright with you, I will put the money into a family trust, and if anybody needs some it is there."

"What will you do with your time," asked Tracy.

"Help bring up Karla, if I'm allowed."

Tracy walked over to him and gave him a kiss. "Of course you are Uncle Mike, I would not have expected otherwise."

They all agreed, making both Mike and Tracy executors of the trust.

Mike subdivided off five acres for himself; then in November 1989, he sold the rest of the Standish Estate.

CHAPTER 27

Just a year later Susan died. Both Mike and Timothy were devastated. Again it was Tracy that helped them both through the pain and loss even though it was her mother, and she had to grieve too. But then she had Karla to care for, and with Martin's help, she coped with it all.

Timothy moved in with Martin and Tracy for a while, but then he had a stroke and with only one arm, it soon became apparent that he was in need of professional care, so they put him into a nursing home with hospital facilities. They all took it in turns to visit him twice a week, then in 1997 at the age of 77, Timothy Standish gave up his fight for life. This time it was Mike who consoled Tracy. Their personal support network that they had created all those years ago still functioned as strong and as well as had ever done.

Mike kept himself busy with a few sheep and chickens, and a goat named Alfred. Tracy and Martin would come out during the school holidays with Karla and they would roam the foothills and valleys chasing rabbits. Much to Mike's disgust, Tracy bought Karla a lamb as a pet and Mike had to care for it most of the time. "They are not meant to be domestic animals" he complained, but Tracy just kissed him. She still had those "puppy dog" eyes that he could not resist. Trouble was Karla had them too. Mike knew he was doomed.

However, Karla brought him more than just the eyes. She told Tracy that she was worried about Uncle Mike being way out in the country without any companion and insisted on getting him a puppy. Tracy was not so sure and decided to check with Mike first. Initially he balked at the idea but when he realised that it was Karla's way of looking after him he accepted. She spent an inordinate amount of time going into every pet shop, looking for just the right dog, but it was from the SPCA that she eventually selected an abandoned Australian Terrier Mongrel cross bitch, nearly a year old. She very proudly presented it to Mike a week later. He named her Jess, and she took to Mike immediately, cuddling up on the armchair beside him and immediately falling asleep.

Karla did not have her mother looks, she wasn't ugly, but was one of those woman that when you look at them for the first time you ask yourself, 'is she attractive or not?' Then as you see her a few more times and get to know her, you suddenly realise that she is.

Over the months and years, Karla grew into a loving caring young woman, who loved Mikes homestead and always insisted they go there at Christmas for the holidays, as well as every other opportunity she could find. Like her mother, Mike found that they had developed a very close bond and he doted over her. Although unsaid Tracy and Mike both knew that this was the baby that he and Paula never had.

As he had done with Tracy, they had heart to heart discussions about anything and everything. When she was just fourteen she asked him about the wedding ring he wore on his finger.

"I didn't know you were ever married," she asked one day.

Mike studied her for a moment. 'Was she too young to hear the truth about Paula?', then he remembered her mother. She had been only sixteen.

Mike started to relate the events that had occurred, all the time watching her reactions, trying to gauge her real interest. He took over an hour. At one point Tracy came out and listened to the conversation for a while, then without a word put her hand on Mike shoulder, gave it a squeeze, and walked away. Karla seemed to hang on every word. She would stop him from time to time to clarify something and showed genuine interest and concern. At times he would see tears appear in her eyes, at other times laughter. He was surprised at the shock on her face when he revealed the truth about Paula, that he now believed the whole episode to be true.

"Have you ever tried to get back in?" she asked looking over to the valley that the tunnel lay in. "It's just over there."

Mike followed her gaze. "Yes at times I have considered it, but after your mother helped me to find the truth, I have been content with that. Maybe one day somebody will find the valley again, maybe somebody has; but I am eighty with a gammy leg. It won't be me."

"But the rail tunnel is unused now, couldn't we look?"

Mike raised his eyebrows. "We?"

"Yes, you know how I love mysteries and solving riddles and clues."

He smiled at her. "You're going to be quite a problem when you get older."

"I'm quite a problem now."

Mike laughed and gave her a hug. "You sure are," he said as they went in for tea.

On the week of Karla's sixteenth birthday they all went to Christchurch on a week's holiday. They explored and did all the things tourists do, and Karla enjoyed every minute. Though at one point they left her alone at the hotel for about an hour. She thought it was a bit strange, especially when they came back. Tracy gave her a hug and said "Happy Birthday darling," with no apparent present, but then they went out to an expensive restaurant and had a wonderful night and she thought no more of it. Mike seemed a little quieter than usual, but happy and more than a little contented.

"Is everything OK Uncle Mike?" Karla asked. "It is now," he said with a smile, and gave her a big hug and a kiss.

It was not long after this when she once again came up and sat down with Mike on what was now accepted as his discussion seat.

"Uncle Mike, I've been thinking."

"Oh oh, why does that scare me," he replied.

She gave him a shove

"Beating up old men too; it gets even worse."

'Uncle Mike," she started again, "Have you any real proof that the valley existed? I mean other that what you discovered at Paula's parents."

"You sound like Tony." He could have been hurt by the inference, and possibly would have been if it had come from anybody else.

Karla half turned to face him and put her hands on his. "I believe that you believe that it is all true. I don't doubt your integrity or your love for Paula. But now it is me that wants to believe like you do. You found your proof, now I want to find mine."

Mike took her hands in his and held them. He looked into her young innocent, enquiring face. This may have been his third cousin by marriage, but to Mike this was his daughter, Paula's surrogate child.

"I wish there was."

"Did she give you anything?"

"No, I gave her my pocket watch, but we exchanged it many times in the cave, and I don't know who had it last. But you see even if I had it, it proves nothing. If she had it, then it is lost with her. If I just lost it then who knows."

Karla lowered her head.

"And there is no other way in?" she said looking up at him again.

"No…" He hesitated. "Well … no" he said finally.

Karla looked at him closely. "Well what," she shot back at him.

"Well I had a feeling, and it may have been totally wrong, that there could have been. BUT …, But it could have lead back into the valley. I don't know, and remember I have lived here all my life. I know these ranges like no one else, and I have never found another entrance."

Karla looked disappointed.

"BUT …" Mike continued, "I know it exists. One day someone will find it again, if they want it hard enough." He suddenly stood up. "Let's get something to drink."

Karla nodded, and stood up with him. He flashed her a quick look, then took her arm in his and walked back to the homestead. Karla said nothing, but the strange glint in his eye had not gone unnoticed.

CHAPTER 28

Chris appeared on the scene when Karla was nearly twenty-one. She brought him out to the farm one Saturday morning.

"Uncle Mike, I want you to meet a friend of mine. This is Chris."

Mike looked him up and down. "I was wondering when I was going to meet you," he said extending his hand.

Chris took it with a firm shake. "It's a pleasure to meet you, Karla often talked about you."

"Well you had better come inside and I will try and correct all her lies."

Mike sat them down in the lounge, then put on the jug and stood in the doorway. Chris and Karla sat on the couch looking at each other and holding hands. Jess as usual snuck up beside her and did her best to be unseen by Mike. She was not allowed on the furniture, but Jess and Karla had formed just as close a bond as Mike and her, so he pretended not to see.

"So," he said giving them both a start. "Tell me about yourself."

"Well my name is Chris Thompson, I was born in 1982, I live …"

"Hang on," cut in Mike. "You sound like you're applying for a job. Little Miss Trouble here has got you all schooled up I bet." He looked at Karla. She screwed up her face and poked her tongue out at him. "I warn you now," Mike added shifting his eyes to Chris. "She is a very organised, intelligent, strong willed, capable, and a powerful force to be reckoned with." Karla opened her mouth to say something, but Mike was too quick. "She is also very loving, caring and empathetic." He raised his finger as her mouth opened again. "She is sensitive and trusting, and the best friend anyone could ever have, believe me I know. Don't ever hurt her." Now Mike looked questioningly at Karla, but she said nothing, a slight shade of red however had crept over her cheeks.

Chris looked up at Mike. "That she also told me. That you would be very protective of her; and I don't blame you. I truly believe all that you said but there's more. A side you haven't seen."

"Really," Mike replied, a little taken aback at his candid answer.

"Yes; she is an old fashioned romantic. You know she won't let me get too close to her, if you know what I mean, until we are…" He hesitated embarrassed as he realised what he had just said "if we are, I mean married. I like that."

"Chris! Mike!" Karla retorted shocked at the direction of the conversation. "You're supposed to be interrogating Chris, not embarrassing me."

"Who says?" they both replied almost in unison.

Karla looked at each of them in turn, doing her best to pout.

Mike just laughed. He knew she was feigning and not really hurt.

Chris however looked a little concerned. He looked at Karla. "Some things are worth waiting for."

The words hit Mike like a hammer blow, and he actually took a step back. "I'll just make a coffee," he said and swung around the corner into the kitchen. He took a deep breath and let it out slowly. He could see Paula standing before him in the cave, as clear as if it were yesterday.

He made the drinks and took them back in setting them on a small round table.

"Karla said that you used to own all the land around here," Chris started in conversation.

"Yea. One thousand acres we had, from the road right back to the range behind us. But now I have five. That's enough for me, too much at times. So where do you come from?"

"I was born in Invercargill; my parents had a business there repairing farm machinery. But they died in a car crash when I was nine. Since then I have lived with my Grandparents in Kaiapoi, just north of Christchurch."

"So how did you two meet?"

"At high school. Then one day about eight months ago we meet on the street, and we sort of got friendly."

"You kept all this quiet," Mike directed his statement at Karla.

"No sense in having the housewarming party, until you have the house."

"And do you have a house?"

"I might be thinking about a conditional offer."

"Conditional?" Chris chipped in.

"Yes, conditional on my current landlords consent."

Mike laughed. "Do you have any idea what you are getting into?"

"Yes, trouble," Chris replied.

Mike showed Chris around the homestead. He felt that he liked this young man.

"What do you do for a job?" he asked.

"I work in the local garage. I only have one more year and I will have completed my apprenticeship."

They spent another two hours talking, and Karla made pancakes for afternoon tea, then around four, she suggested that had better be getting back.

Mike unlatched the front gate and lifted it up on its broken hinge to open it.

"I must get around to fixing that one day."

"I could come out the weekend after next and help you if you like," Chris offered.

Mike was about to decline 'saying she'll be right,' but then decided that if he was going to get to know this man properly, he would need to actually be with him. He also suspected that he was one of those "landlords" Karla had spoken about, so she would also like him to get to know Chris.

"Thank you, that would be appreciated, I'll never get it done otherwise."

"Great, we will see you then."

They shook hands.

Karla came up and put her arms around him. "Thank you Uncle Mike."

CHAPTER 29

It was about ten months later when Mike saw the trail of dust coming up the road, signalling the arrival of Chris and Karla. As usual the car stopped on the verge by the gate and Jess ran down to meet them. Mike sat and waited but they initially did not get out; then Karla got out, slammed the door and stood by the back of the car with her arms folded, and even at that distance Mike could see thunder on her face.

"Oh oh," he said under his breath. "Looks like the inevitable lovers quarrel, better see what I can do."

He got out of his porch chair and made his way towards the car. As he got to the gate, Chris got out and came up to him. They shook hands then they moved back up towards the house.

"I've done a stupid thing," Chris confided in him. "I took some money out of our holiday fund and bought something without telling her." He nodded his head in Karla's direction.

"I hope it was for something important," Mike said quietly.

"Well when she asked, I couldn't tell her. That's when she got really mad." He hesitated, then checking to see that she wasn't looking, slipped his hand into his pocket and pulled out a small box. He flipped it open to reveal a diamond ring. "I mean how could I? Now she will hardly speak to me."

"OK, leave it to me."

Mike left him by the porch and walked up beside Karla.

"Hello Uncle Mike," she said while still looking at the distant hills.

"Hello darling," he replied.

"How could he?" Mike looked at her as a tear rolled down her cheek.

Mike put his arm around her shoulder. "Discussion seat." was all he said.

He led her in through the gate, and round passed the side of the house to the old bench seat, indicating to Chris that he should follow. They sat down with Mike between them.

"You know Karla; I found myself in a similar situation with your mother a number of years ago. She was younger that you, just sixteen if I recall. She made a decision that she truly thought in her heart was the right one. A decision that affected me directly." Karla turned to look at him, and he put his hand on hers. "I could have been very angry with her for it; but I knew her. I trusted her. I knew that whatever her reason, it was not because she wanted to hurt me. I realised that she did it out of love."

"Is that when mum told you about Paula's parents?"

Mike nodded; then continued. "I told her what I am going to tell you now." He turned around to look at Chris.

"Sometimes you do things that you believe is right at the time, for the very best of reasons. Sometimes they work out but sometimes it doesn't go the way you planned. Whatever the outcome you still need to be true to your heart, and accept the consequences." He shifted his look back to Karla again. "It all comes down to trust. I knew that your mother would not do anything to hurt me intentionally. Yes I was annoyed with her at first, but as it turned out, she did the right thing for me. You two," and he put his arm around both their shoulders, "need to learn to trust one another. You need to communicate, to be honest with each other. However there will be the odd occasion when you can't communicate for a good reason.

Then you need to trust the other, even though you didn't understand the reason at that time. Then you need to have faith in them that their intentions are good, even if sometimes obscure, that they do what they do out of love." He looked across at Chris. He was looking at Karla. She in turn was looking at the ground. Mike studied her for a moment. The look of thunder was gone. In fact, she looked slightly ashamed. Mike stood up and walked around the front of Chris. He stopped for a moment and put his hand on Chris's shoulder. Their eyes meet and Mike gave him a slight nod before he made his way up to the homestead.

He heard Chris say behind him "I'm sorry Karla, but I really do have a good reason."

Mike turned around when he got to the back door and looked at the couple. Chris had moved along to sit beside Karla and they were in deep discussion. He saw Chris reach into his pocket. Mike held his breath, then Karla jumped from her seat "Oh Chris, of course I will," he heard her almost shout, and she through her arms around him. As she hugged him, swinging in his arms, she looked over his shoulder and saw Mike watching them. She mouthed him a thank you, and a kiss.

Mike felt his eyes water. "Our little girl is all grown up," he said quietly.

Over the next few months Chris and Karla made regular visits to the farm. Chris helped Mike with little jobs about the place. Mike could have done most of them himself, but he was enjoying his company and he had to admit he was not getting younger. Karla did his washing and ironing and tidied up the house for him, and made lunch for them all.

Arrangements were now underway for the wedding. Karla insisted that it be held out at the farm.

"It is the Standish Tradition," she stated emphatically.

Hotels and motels in Springfield were booked out and a marquee was put on the usual wedding spot. The platform was erected and decorated with flowers.

Mike stood at the back door surveying the scene. This was the fourth wedding to have been held on this spot, and the third Mike had attended, but he knew it would be the last he would see. He sensed someone coming up beside him and felt Tracy slip her arm around his. They held each other's hands in silence for several minutes, each lost in their own thoughts.

"Thank you for being here for us, both me and Karla all these years," she said resting her head on Mike's shoulder. "Especially what you have done for Karla."

"Thank you for letting her be my surrogate daughter. It has meant so much to me."

She squeezed his hand.

Mike looked over to where Karla stood talking to her bridesmaids, out of sight from the gathered throng, obviously giving them last minute instructions. He knew them of course, but not well, only from when she and Chris had held parties at the farm.

Emily was wild and impish, but he liked her more that all the others. Sharon was ordinary, unspectacular but a quiet and friendly girl. She was more the sort that he would have expected Karla to associate with. Then there was Fiona. She was loud and at times could be quite obnoxious, and Mike did not like her much at all. She was the one who surprised him the most as being a friend of Karla's, being so totally different in personality. As Mike watched though, and despite their greatly differing backgrounds, it was obvious that they all had deep respect for Karla, and she had total authority over all of them.

As he had done with Tracy, Mike stood on the platform with her father to give her away. He looked down at the guests, and noted that the seat beside Tracy was vacant. She had organised all the seating, 'was this a coincidence, or on purpose?' he wondered. Later at the reception, he saw the vacant place setting again, and knew the answer.

He looked around again. Most of the guests were young, and he felt out of place, an old grey-haired man, generations apart. Tracy looked up at him, tears of joy in her eyes. She smiled and nodded to give him reassurance. And he appreciated it.

The music started and his attention was drawn to the end of the carpet. Karla now stood there arrayed in white, her bridesmaids assembled behind in pale pink. He leaned on his walking stick as he watched her glide up the aisle towards him; she was a picture of grace and elegance, totally in control of herself and her surroundings. She floated up the steps onto the platform. Mike could now see her face through the veil. A slight smile broached her lips. As she drew level their eyes met. Her smile deepened and she gave him a quick wink. Mike felt his chest swell and his body straightened, and at that moment he had never so proud in all his life. But more than that, he felt a sense of accomplishment, of fulfilment. He felt at peace.

The reception went off without a flaw, not that Mike had any doubts with Tracy and Karla organising things. They received many gifts, but Mike's was special, a fully paid four week honeymoon in Australia, exploring Melbourne and Adelaide, part of which was five days on a river boat on the Murray.

On their return, they rented a little house in Kaiapoi. The families on both sides chipped in with furniture and other items, and along with the wedding presents they had received, they were well set up as a young couple.

Every fortnight Karla and Chris made the trip out to Mike's place to spend time with him and to do any chores that needed doing. Mike was still quite capable but knew that they wanted to do it for him, and so let them, and appreciated their help. He did tend to rattle about in the expanse of the house. Although he only occupied one bedroom the rest of the building still needed attention, so every two months Karla and Chris would stay over and do the whole place. On those occasions Tracy and Martin would often come out, and the whole family would spend the weekend, and the homestead would come alive with noise and merriment as if had in years gone by.

CHAPTER 30

Mike eased himself into his chair. Jess as normal curled up and put her head on his foot.

He was not sure how long he had sat there.

Something seemed to wake him, then he took in a long deep breath, and relaxed.

"Are you ready?" she asked.

Mike looked up at the young woman beside him and smiled happily.

"I've always been ready," he replied.

"Then let's go home." She took him by the hand and he obediently rose from his chair.

The young man hooked his arm around hers, and with his dog at their side, they disappeared into the darkness.

CHAPTER 31

In February 2009, two years after their marriage they prepared as usual to head out to the homestead. They packed up a few tools and by 8am were on their way. The road now was a main highway to the West Coast and in excellent condition. In times past the train had been the fastest way, now however, there was no commuter service. The only passenger service was the now world famous Trans Alpine to Greymouth. But in a race they would still beat it to Springfield. They turned off and headed down the country roads towards the farm, the sealed road eventually turning into metal as they approached the old house.

Pulling up at the gate they saw Mike sitting in his usual chair. Chris turned off the engine and opened the door.

"Chris, something is wrong. Where is Jess?"

Chris looked across at them on the porch.

"Stay here," he said and opened the gate. As he approached he could see that there was no movement from either of them. He walked up to them, they just appeared peacefully asleep. He returned to the car. Karla was standing at the door tears streaming down her face. Chris took her in his arms and they both cried together.

The funeral was a small affair at the Memorial Gardens Crematorium in Christchurch.

Karla had organised it, with the help of Tracy and Chris, and apart from Martin, only a few of the neighbours attended. She took his ashes home in an earthen jar, not really knowing what to do with them, but also not wanting to leave them in a hole somewhere.

It was a few days after the service and cremation, that she received a letter. The letterhead identified its origin as being from a Solicitor, Mr J D Witherspoon. It was addressed directly to her and marked;

"PRIVATE & CONFIDENTIAL"

It read in part;

Dear Mrs Thompson,

As you are a named beneficiary, we request the pleasure of your company at the reading of the Will and Testament of the Late Michael John Standish, at our offices on the 3rd floor of the Stamford Building, 112 Gettings Rd, Christchurch, at 1.30pm on Monday March 16 2009.

Karla handed it to Chris.

"Well we had better go then," he said after reading it.

"I wonder what he would have left me?" She ran through the contents of the homestead in her mind, but could think of nothing that she had ever said she even specifically liked, except the homestead itself, and she could hardly expect that.

At the said date and time, they arrived at the office of Mr Witherspoon.

Strangely, Tracy said she had not got a letter, and even stranger to Karla, she declined to accompany them to the meeting, yet was happy about her going.

His secretary ushered them into a comfortable and spacious room, with a central table and twenty leather bound chairs around it.

"Tea or Coffee?" she asked.

"Tea thank you, milk and one sugar."

"Coffee, white and none," Chris added.

"Mister Witherspoon will be in shortly."

Karla nodded her thanks as the lady went out.

"Are we early, or are the others are very late?" she asked no one in particular.

A door opened at the far end of the room and a middle aged man appeared carrying a manila folder.

"Good afternoon, Mrs Thompson I presume?"

"Yes." Karla replied.

"I'm Jack Witherspoon, please call me Jack. I have been Mike's Solicitor for many years," he paused, "It was very sad to see him go." He sat down on the seat beside her.

She nodded. It was obvious to Karla from his voice, that he really meant it. A knock sounded, and the lady entered with a tray of biscuits and three cups. She put the biscuits in the middle and distributed the cups to the intended recipients.

"Thank you Janice."

"You're welcome," she replied, and left the room.

Jack took a sip of his drink, "Well, shall we start."

"Shouldn't we wait for the others?' Karla interjected.

Jack sat back in his seat and smiled. "There are no others."

Karla shot a look at Chris, and then returned her gaze to Jack, trying to form some words to speak.

"You are the sole beneficiary," he said.

Karla tried to regain some composure. One thing exploded into her mind, "Does that mean we inherit the homestead?" she blurted out.

"The homestead, the land, all his possessions, and a sum of money."

Karla's face lit up, she spun around to Chris, "The homestead." she suddenly got up and hugged him.

"Chris we own Mike's homestead, Oh thank you Mister Witherspoon, thank you Mike, thank you … everyone." She bounced up and down on her toes holding her arms tight against her body.

Chris had to smile at her antics, he knew how much she had loved the place, and he was so happy for her to now own it.

"I think however, you had better sit down for this one," Jack cut into her rapture as he pulled out a piece of paper from the file.

Karla obediently sat, puzzled but still grinning. She looked at the paper as he slid it across to her. It was a bank statement.

"You also inherit this; less duties and taxes of course."

She took it from him, scanning it for a moment. The blood visibly drained from her face, and she looked back at him, her jaw hanging open.

"You see, when Mike sold the farm, he just put the money in an investment. Now it belongs to you."

Karla returned her gaze to the statement. She pushed it to the side so Chris could see also.

"How much?" she stammered.

"I make it just over 3.7 million," Jack replied matter-of-factly, while trying to contain his obvious delight.

It was several minutes before she could speak.

Tears streamed down her face.

"Why me?" she asked. "I'm not even a Standish."

"I have known Mike for many years. He was a real gentleman, and he had a soft spot for you. Said you reminded him of someone very special ... ahh ... P ... Pau ... Paula I think, yes that's it, Paula," he said. "Did you know her?"

Karla and Chris looked at each other a little surprised. She thought back at all those conversations. "Not as well as mum did, but I guess I kind of knew her," she said, stunned, staring at the statement in disbelief.

They sat in silence for a long time.

"You really loved the old man, didn't you?" Chris said.

"Yes, he was a wonderful man, but this?"

"I don't understand why some people found him a bit strange? I mean some thought he went a bit nuts after being trapped in that tunnel, and I guess he did do some strange things at times," he continued.

"Like what?" Karla replied a little defensively.

"No, no, I'm not putting him down or anything, but I mean he never got married, yet he wore a wedding ring. He celebrated a wedding, and birthday of some imaginary woman …"

"She wasn't imaginary, she existed. Mum was at her parent's funeral."

Chris thought for a minute. "But didn't she die two years before Mike's accident? I loved the old man too. He could be a bit eccentric though. They say that the accident affected him mentally. I mean to give away all this." He looked at Jack.

"I admit I know all the stories, but I can assure you he was perfectly sane. You may be interested to know Karla, that you were no afterthought. The day you turned sixteen, Mike sat down here, in this office with your mother and father, and told them that this was what he wanted for you. It was agreed upon unanimously."

Karla looked at him shocked, then slowly started to nod her head and smiled with inner understanding.

They sat in silence for a few more moments, then she raised her head, the smile gone, replaced with sadness.

"Yes I know those stories too," Karla replied. "But he told me a lot about her, and their story. I think he confided in me more than anyone, other than my mum, and I know she believed it all to be true. She was so real, at least to him, and surely that is all that matters. He died happy in his belief of her, real or not."

"So do you belief him?"

Karla thought for a few moments. "I really don't know. The detail and his passion make me really want to, but again there is no physical proof. How could such a place exist without people knowing about it? However mum was much closer to him. She is still totally convinced, and her judgment is impeccable. I don't know, I really don't," she said again.

"Well you're right about one thing. He was a real gentleman, and hey, look what he has done for you." Chris nodded at the statement.

"For us," Karla corrected him, giving him a hug.

"Well I have some paper work here for you to sign, and then you can go off and celebrate. Celebrate his life, he would like that, Oh and he left a letter for you too," Jack handed it to her.

"Thank you, I'll read it later."

Karla did the paperwork in a daze, then, when they had finished, she put the envelope in her bag and stood up.

"Thank you for your assistance Mister Witherspoon, Jack I mean, it was nice meeting you."

"That's OK; it has been a real pleasure."

They shook hands.

Chris opened the door to leave.

"Oh yes, Karla. I almost forgot. The coroner asked me to give you this. He had to prize it from Mike's fingers." Jack reached into his pocket.

Chris was startled by a crash, and he turned to see Karla's purse, its contents strewn about the floor.

Karla however, was transfixed; frozen; staring at what lay in Jacks hand.

"What is it?" Chris asked anxiously.

Seconds passed; but it was Jack who spoke; also a little shocked at Karla's reaction.

"It's just an old pocket watch, with a dog's head embossed on it."

WATCH OUT!!!!

For the sequel of this intriguing story as Karla takes up Mike's quest, to find out the truth about Kennard's Valley.

In;

"The Search for Kennard's Valley"

GLOSSARY

Crib

A small dwelling often by a beach. A New Zealand term, specific to the South Island.

In the North Island it is called a Bach, or in other countries a holiday home, beach house or a lake house.

They are an iconic part of New Zealand history and culture, especially in the middle of the 20th century, where they symbolized the beach holiday lifestyle that was becoming more accessible to the middle class.

Glow-worms

The common name for various groups of insect larvae and adult females that glow through bioluminescence.

Jigger

Also known as a handcar, pump trolley, pump car, velocipede or Kalamazoo. A typical design consists of an arm that pivots, seesaw-like, on a base, which the passengers alternately push down and pull up to move the car.

Kahikatea

A coniferous tree, endemic to New Zealand.

Kōkopu

A common name used for three species of fish of the genus Galaxias. They are found in the rivers, lakes and swamps of New Zealand for which they are endemic.

Macrocarpa

Commonly known as Monterey Cypress, is a species of cypress that is endemic to the Central Coast of California.

Pittosporum

A genus of about 200 species of flowering plants in the family Pittosporaceae. The species are trees and shrubs growing to 2-30 m tall. The leaves are spirally arranged or whorled, simple, with an entire or waved (rarely lobed) margin. The flowers are produced singly or in umbels or corymbs, each flower with five sepals and five petals; they are often sweetly scented.

Podocarp

Podocarpaceae is a large family of mainly Southern Hemisphere conifers, comprising about 156 species of evergreen trees and shrubs.

Rimu

Dacrydium cupressinum, commonly known as rimu, is a large evergreen coniferous tree endemic to the forests of New Zealand. It is a member of the southern conifer group, the podocarps. The former name "red pine" has fallen out of common use.

Tawa

The Tawa tree (Beilschmiedia tawa) is a New Zealand broadleaf tree common in the central parts of the country.

Toetoe

Five species of tall grasses native to New Zealand and members of the Austroderia genus.

Totara

Podocarpus totara (tōtara) is a species of podocarp tree endemic to New Zealand.

Tui

The tui (Prosthemadera novaeseelandiae) is an endemic passerine bird of New Zealand. It is one of the largest members of the diverse honeyeater family.

Whiteywood

Melicytus ramiflorus (Māhoe or whiteywood) is a small tree of the family Violaceae endemic to New Zealand.
It grows up to 10 metres high with a trunk up to 60 cm in diameter, it has smooth, whitish bark and brittle twigs.

Source of information - Wikipedia

www.ingramcontent.com/pod-product-compliance
Lightning Source LLC
Chambersburg PA
CBHW030414020726
47493CB00003B/1063